D1564513

# Sharpe Mind: Hanging by a Thread

**Maycroft Mysteries, Volume 3**

Lisa B. Thomas

Published by Cozy Stuff and Such, 2019.

# Copyright

SHARPE MIND

Copyright © 2016 Lisa B. Thomas

Published by Cozy Stuff and Such, LLC

# Prologue

U sually the last gulp of hot coffee would chase away all of Tonya Webber's worries. Not today. In all her twenty-seven years on earth, this was the worst mess she had ever gotten herself into. And she had been in plenty of messes.

Pushing aside the dirty plate and chipped coffee mug, she cleared a space on the diner's red vinyl tablecloth. It was hard to find a spot that was neither sticky with a week's worth of maple syrup nor torn from a lifetime's worth of wear. She pulled a manila folder out of her tote bag and laid it open. Thumbing through the glossy photos, she found the one she wanted. Tears threatened to well in her bottom lids, but she willed them back the same way she had learned to keep back fear and anxiety and regret.

What a beauty. Some would call her stunning. She had a love-hate relationship with her stage costumes. She loved the admiration she got from the audience, especially the jealous women who were second-guessing themselves for agreeing to let their husbands see the show. But she hated how her calves ached at the end of a two-show night.

She had discovered that the real trick of being a Las Vegas showgirl was not the ability to dance. It was learning to balance the heavy headpieces laden with plumes and jewels while strutting around in six-inch heels. Unlike the one-piece costumes of the sixties when Las Vegas was in its heyday, the only thing that distinguished her from a stripper was the headpiece.

Her body looked fabulous in the deep blue rhinestone bikini. Every little girl's dream was to play dress-up. To strut around and be admired. And for a handful of years, she had lived that dream. Then she fell in love, blinked, and it was all gone.

She never thought she would miss it this much.

Just a month ago, she was a star. Men adored her. Woman despised her. Now, brushing back her long black hair, knowing it had lost its luster, she glanced down at the old t-shirt and faded jeans she had thrown on when she and Roscoe snuck out of the flea bit motel they'd been staying at the past week. Dumb jerk, she thought, remembering how easy it was to convince the pimple-faced boy at the front desk not to make her pay for the room in advance. All she had to do was flash a little cleavage, lean over the counter, and bat her fake eyelashes.

That was her real talent—manipulating people. Many times, it had gotten her what she wanted. Other times, it had gotten her in trouble. That's how she ended up here in this run-down dive on the outskirts of Maycroft, Texas. If only she hadn't listened to Roscoe. She'd still be in Vegas instead of running from a bounty hunter in the middle of Hicksville, USA.

Clara walked up with a fresh pot of coffee. "Can I refill your cup, miss?"

Tonya jumped, her thoughts clouding her vision. She hadn't seen the gray-haired waitress teeter up to the table.

"No thanks." She quickly shut the folder, but not before Clara got a glimpse of Tonya wearing her plumes and rhinestone leotard.

"Say, are you one of them ladies?" Clara pointed a bony finger to the folder.

Tonya reached for her bag and stuck the folder back inside. "I was. Not anymore."

Clara brightened as she set down the coffee pot and stuffed her plump body into the booth across from Tonya. "I've been waiting for someone like you to come along these parts. Last one we had here left about ten years ago. She was awfully *mysteeeeer-ious*."

Tonya stared back, confused as to why the old woman was showing such an interest in her.

Clara reached into the pocket of her stained white uniform and pulled out a twenty-dollar bill. She slid it across the table. "Here. Will you do it?"

Tonya's confusion quickly turned up a few degrees. "Just what is it you think I'll do for twenty dollars, lady? I'm not a—"

"Tell me my fortune, of course. You're a fortune teller, ain't ya?" She motioned to the folder.

Tonya looked down at her bag. The old kook must have seen the picture of her and assumed she was a psychic. She tossed a mischievous look across the table. "Sure, I'll tell you your future. Close your eyes."

Clara did as instructed, wiggling with anticipation and clasping her well-aged hands in her lap.

Tonya glanced around to make sure no one was looking and leaned over to pull a five spot out of Clara's pocket. It had been dangling there since the woman had gotten out the twenty. Tonya crinkled it into her hand. "I see money."

"*Oooh*," Clara squealed. "Am I getting rich?"

"No. Lost money." Tonya stifled a laugh at her own cleverness. "You'll lose money today."

"Oh dear." Clara sat with her eyes still squished tight. "Don't you see anything good?"

Tonya glanced out the window. Her boyfriend Roscoe was walking toward the diner from the mechanics shop just down the highway. "Yes. I see a tall, handsome man. He's just your type."

"Really? That's better." Clara opened her eyes and blinked.

Tonya grabbed her bag and slid from the booth. She headed out the door, leaving the five-dollar bill on the table. It was barely enough to cover the coffee and toast, much less a tip.

She leaned against the side of the building and lit a cigarette. When Roscoe walked up, she moved in close, whispering instructions. He waited for her to walk around the back of the diner so she could peek through the window on the other side. She rubbed a clean place on the glass and watched as he opened the door and walked straight toward Clara. He leaned down to kiss her cheek and then gave it a little pinch.

As he walked out the door, Tonya blew out a long stream of smoke. She could see the poor, pathetic waitress blushing, a stupid grin wrinkling up her face. She hadn't even noticed Roscoe slip the five-dollar bill off the table and into his pocket.

# Chapter 1

The **five members** of the Maycroft City Council listened as Bob Chessman presented the Chamber of Commerce's latest plan to increase tourism and bring new business to the small town. As usual, Mayor Bradley Thornhill wore a dark suit and tie along with a paisley pocket square to complete his upper crust, overdressed look. The other members—all men—wore plaid button-down shirts and jeans, a Texan's uniform, of sorts. All had on cowboy boots. It was spring, after all, and no one liked getting their socks soaked trampling through mud puddles along rain-drenched roads.

Deena Sharpe sat on the far aisle in one of the metal folding chairs used to convert the conference room into a meeting hall when the council convened twice a month. Her reporter's notebook looked more like an artist's sketchpad as she doodled faces, birds, dogs, cats, and horses, waiting for something—*anything*—newsworthy. This was definitely not the exciting life of an investigative reporter she had imagined when she quit her teaching job after thirty-three years.

As the rookie political reporter for the *Northeast Texas Tribune*, she quickly learned that long, tiresome meetings were part and parcel of the job. She had developed quite a skill for appearing interested in the proceedings, a trick she'd picked up watching her students in her former career as a high school journalism teacher. First, she would look up from her notepad, tilt her head and bob it a few times. Then she'd scribble out her grocery list, honey-do list for Gary, or inventory list for her booth at the antique mall. Only after all her lists were complete did she resort to mindless doodling.

She stifled a yawn.

Finally, after several failed attempts at Robert's Rules of Order, the mayor let Bob Chessman get on to "new business."

"We feel it's time to put a fresh face on Maycroft," Chessman said. "Jazz it up a little. Therefore, we propose a change to the town's slogan."

"I didn't know we had a town slogan," Marty Fisk said.

Mayor Thornhill banged his gavel. "You're out of order, Councilman Fisk. This is not the time for open discussion. Also, both of you owe a quarter to the donation jar for calling Maycroft a 'town' instead of a 'city.' How will we ever raise our standing if we don't think big?"

"Pipe down, Brad." Before the mayor could slam his gavel again, Fisk added, "I meant '*Mayor* Brad.'"

Deena chuckled under her breath. This kind of contentious banter was par for the course in small-town meetings. She looked around the room to see if others in the audience were amused. Turnout today was even smaller than usual, probably because of the rain. Several elderly women were working on their crochet pieces, and a man with a wooden cane was reading a paperback novel. No one appeared to take much interest in the meeting itself.

Chessman cleared his throat. "As I was saying, we propose to change the city's slogan. Currently, it is, 'Maycroft: The Capital of Quaint.' By the way, Marty, it's on the big sign when you drive into town on the highway. You can't miss it."

Fisk shrugged his shoulders.

Chessman continued. "We have three choices to present. The Council can vote on the one they like best. Your first choice is, 'Maycroft: Quaint We Ain't.'"

Deena watched the reactions of the council members. Blank stares seemed to indicate confusion. She had learned to discriminate the "confusion" stares from the "apathy" and the "I wish I were anywhere else but here" stares.

"That's a joke, right?" Mayor Thornhill asked.

"No sir. Like I said, we want to spruce up our image. Make it more modern."

The mayor glanced down the row of members.

Deena made a note of the first suggestion. First time this group has ever been unanimous on anything.

"Well, maybe you'll like this one." Chessman paused for effect. "It is, 'Maycroft: Better, not Bigger.'"

"Next!" Mayor Thornhill yelled, without even bothering to poll the panel.

"I saved the best for last. This is my personal favorite." Chessman picked up a roll of butcher paper and removed the rubber band. He unfurled the banner. "Here it is. 'Maycroft: The Funshine Town.' Get it? *Fun* shine, not sunshine?"

Mayor Thornhill slammed down his gavel a second time. "There you go calling it a town again, Bob. How many times—"

"We didn't think 'Funshine City' sounded as good!" He waved the banner from one side of the room to the other, looking at the council members for support.

"More like 'The Town Where Fun Goes to Die,'" Fisk said under his breath.

The man in the audience who had been reading let out a low chuckle, banging his cane on the floor. One of the councilmen picked up the sentiment. Soon, almost everyone in the room was laughing so loudly that the mayor's gavel was barely audible over the din. He blustered out, "Order!" over and over.

Bob Chessman quickly rolled up the paper and wadded it into a ball. He, too, was not laughing.

Mayor Thornhill finally gained control. "Mr. Chessman, we appreciate the efforts of you and your staff, but I don't believe the Council is ready to vote on this matter."

"Can I say something now?" Fisk glared down the table at Thornhill.

"Not yet. I want to make a motion." Mayor Thornhill sat up straight and fluffed his pocket hankie. "I propose we hold a contest for a new town slogan—*city* slogan," he said, correcting himself quickly. "Let's ask the residents to submit suggestions. We, the Council, will ultimately make the final decision, of course. Doesn't that sound like fun?"

A few of the members nodded their heads in agreement.

"Is there a second to my motion?" The mayor stared at Councilman Dwyer, who nodded like a dashboard dachshund.

"I'll take that as a yes."

"I got something to say," Fisk said, his tone defiant.

"You may proceed. The matter is now open for discussion."

"How in tarnation is any of this going to do a darned thing to bring more money into this place? I got several businesses to keep afloat and no rinky-dink slogan is going to make one bit of difference. The Chamber of Commerce is supposed to bring in business, not write jingles. Now if you would just approve my plan to re-zone the south side of town—"

"You're out of order, Councilman Fisk. This is time for discussion on *this* motion only. Besides, we've voted down your re-zoning plan three times now. You can't make people sell their homes and move if they don't want to. We're not that kind of town."

The other councilmen grinned at the mayor's faux pas.

He stood up, reached into his pants pocket to retrieve a quarter, and plunked it into the jar on the table. "Besides, a new business opened up a month ago. Maycroft now has its very own mind reader. Or is it fortune teller?"

Fisk banged on the table. "That's not a business! That's a con artist and his sister trying to scam people out of money. I should know. They're working out of one of my rental houses."

"You're out of order again, Councilman Fisk! Now, if there is no more discussion on the motion to hold a slogan contest, we'll call for the vote. All in favor, say 'aye.'"

A less-than-enthusiastic majority cast their vote.

"All opposed, say "nay."

"Not just nay, but *h–*"

"Marty! There are women present!" Mayor Thornhill waved his gavel toward the audience.

Marty Fisk nearly turned over his chair as he stood up and walked out.

Thornhill ignored him. "The 'ayes' have it. Meeting adjourned."

As the mayor banged his gavel one last time, Deena felt a new level of tension in the air. She had a feeling a story was brewing, and it just stormed out the door.

FIVE STRAIGHT DAYS of rain had put a damper on most everything in Maycroft. Tuesday's city council meeting wasn't the only place with low turnout. Businesses saw fewer customers as most shoppers stayed indoors.

After leaving the meeting, Deena pulled up to her friend's thrift shop. There were no signs of life inside. But Sandra's car was out front and the "Open" sign beckoned Deena to slosh through the rain-drenched parking lot to go check it out.

The jingle of the bell on the door brought Sandra out from the storeroom to greet her customer. Then she saw Deena. "Oh, it's just you."

Deena grinned and walked back to the counter. "Well, that's a fine howdy-do."

"You know what I mean," Sandra said. "I was hoping for a flood of customers. No pun intended."

Deena was in her late fifties; Sandra was fifteen years her junior. Still, they had a lot in common and had become good friends. Since retiring from teaching, Deena often stopped by on her way to the newspaper office. The shop was a great place to find treasures for her antique booth, and Sandra always had a pot of hot coffee brewing.

"Where's your umbrella?" Sandra asked.

"Sadly, another one bit the dust. That wind we had on Sunday turned it inside out and broke it. Got any here?"

Sandra led the way to the display of accessories. "I think there's a few left. Just don't–"

"Open them inside. I remember. Last time you nearly passed out when I did that."

Sandra laughed as she picked up a child's umbrella featuring Dora the Explorer. "Then you know I've tested them, and they all work."

Sandra's cell phone rang, and she headed back to the counter to answer it.

Deena debated her choices. One was a black stick model with a curved handle. The other was a white fold-up with skulls and crossbones. She looked around for any others that might have been set down on another shelf. No such luck. She picked up the white one and took it to the register.

"That was Ian," Sandra said. "He has to work late. Looks like soup-for-one tonight."

"I thought lawyers kept bankers' hours?"

"He used to before he left the firm. Now that he's on his own, he sometimes has to work crazy hours."

"He's a good man. Defending the rights of the little guy. So, why don't you come out with Gary and me? We're breaking tradition and going to Las Abuelas tonight instead of on Friday."

Sandra furrowed her brow. "Are you sure that's wise? You're not only breaking tradition—which is bad luck—but you're buying that evil looking umbrella."

Deena laughed as she opened her purse. "Luckily, I'm not as superstitious as you. What do you say?"

Sandra stared intently at the counter.

Deena knew Sandra's superstitious nature ran deep, but she'd never seen it trouble her like this. "What if I promise to leave the haunted umbrella at home?"

Shaking her head, Sandra declined. "I know you think I'm just being silly, but I can't help it. I've just always believed in signs and spirits and such. I think I'll stay home tonight and wait on Ian for dinner."

"Suit yourself. And I don't think you're silly. We all have our quirks."

"Like how you can't get through a meal without spilling something on yourself?"

Deena clucked as she reached for her wallet. "I didn't think anyone noticed."

"Hey, I'm not taking money for that awful thing. I'm glad to see it leave the shop." She pushed a large jar to the front of the counter. "You are welcome to make a donation to the animal shelter, though."

Deena stuffed a ten-dollar bill inside. "By the way, my visit isn't just personal. Since you know everybody in town, I was wondering what you could tell me about Marty Fisk."

"Marty? He's on the City Council." Sandra walked back toward the storeroom and motioned for Deena to follow.

"I know. I just left today's meeting. He's all fired up about re-zoning the south side of town. Any idea why?"

Sandra handed Deena a cup of hot coffee, blowing steam off the top of her own. "Besides owning the pawn shop, he has a bunch of rental properties. Rumor has it he wants to build a big commercial office complex."

"What's stopping him?"

"There's a few hold-outs in that area of town who won't sell their property."

"I see." Deena felt the warm brew travel down her insides. "So if the city re-zones, would they have to move?"

"I guess. I haven't paid much attention to what they've been doing since Brad Thornhill got elected mayor. He knows as much about running a municipality as I do about building a rocket ship." She headed back to the store's front counter.

Deena drummed her un-manicured nails against the side of the cup. "It was obvious at the meeting that he and Fisk don't see eye-to-eye on the re-zoning issue. I think I'm going to talk to some of the residents. Looks like there may be a story here."

A loud thump came from the storeroom.

Deena flinched, almost spilling her coffee. "What was that?"

Sandra glanced back over her shoulder and let out a sigh. "I think my storage closet is haunted."

Deena laughed as she pulled the price tag off her new umbrella. "Yeah. I'm sure that's it."

"No, I'm serious. I've heard noises like that a couple of times this week. Couldn't figure out where they were coming from. Then I realized it was coming from the storage closet where I keep clothes of the newly deceased." She wiped her hand slowly across the counter. "Then it made sense."

"What? The newly deceased?" Deena glanced at her watch. "I'm sure it's just a mouse or a squirrel. Have you called an exterminator?"

"No. I'm getting used to it. Besides, Sister Natasha said I have spirits all around me."

"Sister who? Is she a nun?"

"She's that new psychic reader on Fourth Street."

Deena squinted her eyes, trying to make sense of what Sandra was saying. "Look, sorry to run out like this, but I've got a meeting with Lloyd back at the office." She buttoned the front of her red raincoat. "This conversation isn't over, though. Call Bugs-Be-Gone. I'm sure it's just a rat. I'll see you later."

The jingling of the bells behind her on the front door made Deena uneasy. She recalled a story she used to tell her students about the expression, "saved by the bell." Legend had it that some people used to be buried with a string tied from their finger to a bell positioned above the grave, just in case it turned out they had been buried alive. Was Sandra's superstitious nature rubbing off on her?

She ducked under her new umbrella just as the door slammed behind her. That was loud. Loud enough to wake the dead.

# Chapter 2

An aluminum saucepan sat in the middle of the kitchen floor catching a constant drip of rain from the ceiling. A trashcan served the same purpose in the hallway where several chunks of ceiling plaster had given way to the constant stream of water.

Roscoe Trainor paced the floor of the kitchen like a caged animal, his cell phone at his ear.

Tonya stepped around the pan to get to the refrigerator. "He still hasn't answered?" She stared inside at the pathetic offerings. A box of American cheese, a half-empty quart of milk, a couple of cans of beer, and some old lunch meat that may or may not have gone bad stared back at her. "We need more paper towels." She reached for a beer and popped the top.

"Keeps going to voicemail. Don't worry. I'll call Fisk at the pawn shop when it opens at ten. If he doesn't get someone out to fix these leaks today, I'll personally drag him back here myself."

Tonya flinched. She had, on occasion, seen Roscoe's dark side. Besides being one of the most devious, talented con artists this side of the Mason-Dixon, he had a temper. Luckily, it had never reared its ugly head toward her.

"Why aren't you dressed yet?" He checked the time on his watch.

She picked up the least-bruised piece of fruit from the bowl. Beer and bananas. Breakfast of champions. "Do you really think anyone is going to drag through the mud and the rain to see a psychic on a day like this?"

"Maybe not, but you never know." He adjusted the knot on his necktie and tucked in his white dress shirt.

Even dressed like a butler, Roscoe was the handsomest man she'd ever seen. Still, she wished she didn't have to rely on him for everything these days.

The one time she ventured into town in her psychic getup, the stares and whispers were too much for her to take. It seemed unfair that even though he was the one on the lam, she felt like the one hiding out. "When are you going to the market? I'm starving." She took a bite of banana.

"After dark, as always." He walked through the makeshift curtained divider they had constructed between the front room and the rest of the house. He hung his suit jacket on the coat rack next to the front door.

"It's dark already because of this stupid rain. It never rained in Vegas." Tonya slumped down in the kitchen chair and propped her feet up on the crosspiece of the wooden table.

Roscoe rubbed her shoulders. "I'm sorry, babe. I know you've been stuck in the house for weeks. You just have to be patient." He pulled off the towel she had wrapped around her head and leaned down to kiss her cheek. "Just a few more months and we should have enough money for our new IDs and passports. Then it's goodbye rainy Texas. Hello sunny Mexico."

She sat for a moment pouting. "How much money do we have?"

He stopped the shoulder massage. "I haven't counted lately."

He was avoiding her question, as usual. "After you paid the mechanic, how much money did we have left?" She took his hand and pulled him around to sit in the chair across from her.

"Don't worry yourself with the details. I've got it all worked out." He pulled out his cell phone and opened a YouTube video. "You just need to keep working on that accent. Yesterday, it sounded more like East Texas than Eastern Europe.

She dropped her head. "Not Rocky and Bullwinkle again! At least find a different episode of that stupid cartoon."

"Okay, but those customers out there have to think Sister Natasha sounds like Natasha Fatale if they are going to keep handing over their cash." He gave her the phone and smiled.

Although she was pretending to be a fortune teller, she might as well be a mind reader. He never gave her a straight answer when it came to money. Too bad she was such a sucker for his charm. More than that, though, he was her best chance of getting to Mexico with enough money to locate Michael.

# Chapter 3

The *Northeast Texas Tribune* newspaper came out three days a week and covered news across several counties. Local advertising supported the cost of publication. However, with more and more people accessing their news online and through social media, Managing Editor Lloyd Pryor was looking for ways to cut costs.

Walking through the doors of the old brick warehouse that housed the newspaper offices, Deena thought about whether her job could be on the line. Last hired; first fired. She had gone to work the previous fall as a part-time reporter covering local politics. Only a few of her stories had garnered any real attention.

But she knew Lloyd appreciated her maturity, and her meager salary surely wouldn't make a dent in the budget. Even though being a "real reporter" hadn't been as fulfilling as she had hoped, she liked the idea of being on staff.

Luckily, she still had her antique booth to keep her busy. Financially, she and Gary would be fine. They had no children and could manage without her piddlin' paycheck, if necessary.

Bert, the newspaper's copy editor, stood next to Lloyd's desk as she waited outside the office. From the sound of it,

Lloyd was giving him a good chewing out over a typo that appeared in that day's issue.

She had snickered and shown it to Gary over morning coffee. The lead story on the sports page read: "Maycroft HS Soccer Team Scores Two Girls to Take Title."

Gary had read it and said, "Things sure have changed since we were in school."

Spotting Deena in the doorway, Lloyd dismissed Bert who rushed past, looking anxious to get out of the line of fire.

Deena walked in and sat in a cushy chair in the corner. She dropped her tote bag on the floor and asked, "What's *news*, boss?"

"Not today. I'm not in the mood." He moved folders across his desk and threw a wad of paper toward the trashcan. He missed.

By now, Deena had become used to her boss's mood swings. He lived and died by typos. She waved her hand. "Don't worry. I'm sure no one even noticed."

The phone on his desk rang, and he snatched up the receiver. "Uh-huh. Yes. Thanks." He smashed it back on the cradle. "Right. That's at least the hundredth call I've gotten today." He punched some buttons on the console, attempting to put the phone on hold.

"Aww, c'mon. Journalists aren't supposed to use hyperbole."

He leaned back in his chair. "What do you want?"

"You scheduled a meeting with me, remember?" She tapped her foot nervously as she waited for him to answer the phone again. His coffee-stained tie showed at least three spills, and it was barely eleven o'clock.

This time he unplugged the cord in the back. "Sorry. Bad morning."

He pulled his glasses from the top of his head and fumbled for the right notepad on his desk. "I know you are aware of the paper's financial difficulties. Unfortunately, I'm going to have to make some changes."

Deena leaned down to pick up her handbag for security. Even though she knew it was a possibility, the reality of getting laid off made her swallow hard. She braced herself.

"I need you to start writing features. I'm re-assigning your political beat." He looked over the top of his glasses.

Her jaw dropped as her bag slipped to the ground.

"I know it's not what you want, but Laurie's about to go on maternity leave. I need someone to replace her. Dan can handle your beat along with police news."

"Dan Carson?" Deena found her voice. "As long as he can cover it from a stool at Grady's Sports Bar."

"Now, now. He's a good reporter." Pryor looked at his notes. "It's not permanent. Just until things pick up in the fall. I'm trying to find a new marketing manager who can help us with our online presence."

Deena let out a sigh, not sure if she should be relieved or not. "What online presence?"

"Exactly." Lloyd stood up and picked up several balls of paper around the trashcan. "Go talk to Laurie and see what she's working on. Maybe you'll be interested." He offered up a half-hearted smile.

Features. Garden parties and church socials. Sure, she was bored with her beat, but at least it was real news. It seemed like she was taking a step backward rather than forward.

"Alright. As long as it's temporary." She headed for the door. "By the way, I have a lead that might turn out to be something."

"Can you write a feature on it?"

"Sure. Maybe." Not really. She left the office dragging her feet. So much for being an investigative reporter.

# Chapter 4

The small bathroom in the rental house had one thing going for it. There was enough counter space for Tonya to lay out all the make-up she used to transform from Tonya Webber, Arkansas native turned Las Vegas showgirl, to Sister Natasha, Eastern European gypsy fortune teller. That was as deep as her new backstory went. Thus far, she hadn't needed to explain why she and her "brother" had decided to take up residence in Maycroft. Roscoe had told Marty Fisk she was his sister, not knowing if he'd rent to an unmarried couple.

Roscoe stepped into the doorway. "Are you ready?"

"Almost. How's my make-up?" She gave a sultry look to the mirror, batting her dark eyes with their thick, fake lashes and heavy eyeliner. Her look was mysterious and exotic, a talent she had learned from her time on the stages of Las Vegas. She accented her face in such a way that her cheeks appeared sunken. She puckered her crimson lips.

"Perfect." He handed her the long scarf she wore draped around her head turban-style, letting her long, wavy locks fall past her shoulders. He straightened her fringed shawl.

She pulled on the last of her cheap silver bangles and chunky rings. Over-sized hoop earrings provided the finishing touch. "I'm ready."

She picked up Roscoe's cell phone and headed to the bedroom to sit in the house's only comfortable chair. She touched the button to play and once again found herself immersed in "The Rocky and Bullwinkle Show."

But instead of practicing her Natasha accent, Tonya closed her eyes and thought about the day at the diner when she and Roscoe first concocted their scheme. They had needed money. Badly. When they left Las Vegas, all they had was fifteen-hundred dollars in cash. They had spent the rest of their combined savings to pay Roscoe's bail. It was his third arrest for pick pocketing, and they knew this latest charge would lead to jail time. Tonya couldn't let that happen. She gave her life's savings to Atlas Bail Bonds, and they took off the next day.

When she had relayed to him the incident at the café with the unsuspecting waitress, a light bulb had gone off in his head. They would bilk the quaint town of Maycroft to get the money they needed to hide out in Mexico. By the end of that day, they had secured the sparsely furnished rental house from Marty Fisk. By the end of that week, they had bought costumes from a thrift store and were ready to hang their shingle. As always, Roscoe had performed his magic.

As long as they could keep their true identities secret and the cash flowing, they would be able to steal away to Mexico and say "adios" to all their troubles.

Tonya pictured herself with long, tanned legs stretched out on a beach chair, sipping a cocktail with one of those paper umbrellas in it. Roscoe would only have eyes for her. She, on the other hand, would be searching for someone else. Someone who had slipped away from her years earlier.

The buzzer sounded on the front door, making her jump.

Roscoe stuck his head in the bedroom. "Someone's here." He reached for his upper lip and mashed down the fake mustache.

Tonya took one last look in the mirror and waited in the kitchen with the lights out. Showtime.

She peeked through a hole they had made in the curtain as Roscoe sprang into action. He lit the candles on the small square table in the front parlor and turned off the lamp.

The buzzer rang again. He opened the front door.

It was Betty Donaldson, the librarian. This was her third visit.

"Come in, please." Roscoe spoke with a baritone voice.

Betty shook the water off her umbrella before stepping inside. Roscoe took her coat and hung it up, placing the umbrella on the floor. He moved slowly and methodically, further adding to the creepy ambience. Closing the front door, he held out his hand and then stashed the bills she gave him in his pocket. "Follow me." He walked toward the table and pulled out a chair. "Wait."

They had arranged the front room in such a way that the customer would sit in the corner with her back to the curtain, facing toward the front door. Tonya, dressed as Natasha, would sit across the table. More often than not, the customer—always a woman—would set her handbag down on the shabby, carpeted floor next to her. That made it easy for Roscoe to reach through a slit in the curtain to take out—or slip in—whatever he wanted.

Sometimes he thought his mastery of sleight of hand was being wasted on this con. In order to keep up his skills, he would pickpocket at least one unsuspecting shopper every time he hit the market.

He walked around the curtain on the far side of the room. "Do you have the cards?"

Tonya felt the pocket of her flowing skirt and nodded.

He mouthed the words "bad news."

Didn't she give the librarian bad news last time she was here? No matter. Roscoe would take care of it.

He pulled back a small opening in the curtain and announced, "*Sis-ter Na-ta-sha.*"

Tonya swept into the room, gliding into the chair like a buzzard coming in for a landing. She laid her palms flat on the table and closed her eyes, slowly rocking back and forth. She felt the heat from the candle on her face. Slowly, she opened her eyes as if coming out of a deep slumber. At last, she spoke in her best foreign accent. "You come again to see Sister Natasha. Why?"

Betty swallowed hard and leaned in. "I want to know if my husband is having an affair?"

Tonya started to laugh. Of course, he was! Hadn't she looked in the mirror lately? Somehow, she managed to turn her laugh into a weird wailing sound, covering her face with her hands in order to hide her grin. Betty sat back, frightened by the outburst. She pushed her glasses further up on her nose.

Tonya regained her composure. "Natasha consult cards." She pulled the deck of playing cards from her pocket and set them on the table. "Mix."

Betty's hands trembled as she obeyed the command.

Tonya stared as the woman swirled the cards around on the table. She seemed nervous. That was a good sign.

When they first started this scheme, Roscoe had tried to get Tonya to use the tarot cards he carried in his box of tricks. But she could never remember what each card meant. After several failed attempts, she resorted to using a regular deck of playing cards and doing it her own way. After all, she had worked part-time as a dealer in a sleazy casino before landing a job as a dancer.

That's where she met Roscoe. He worked as a magician in the same casino, playing three shows a day. She fell for him the moment they met.

Betty set the deck in the center of the table.

Tonya picked it up and placed two cards face down in front of Betty. She laid several cards face up. With each one, she mumbled a sound to signify a different emotion. Finally, she turned over the two cards in front of Betty.

"No!" Tonya quickly scooped up all the cards and placed them back on the deck.

"What is it? Is he cheating?" Betty's anxious eyes craved an answer.

Tonya decided to give the poor woman a break. After all, it wasn't her fault she wasn't born beautiful. She could use a makeover, however. "Natasha sees no husband cheating." She crossed her arms and set her jaw.

"Ah. That's a relief." Betty put her hand to her chest. "But you did see something, right?"

"Natasha sees what she sees."

"What? What is it?"

Tonya hesitated, knowing Betty was hanging on her every word. "Natasha sees bad fortune. Bad luck." She sucked in an exaggerated breath. "Now, go."

Betty appeared frozen in place.

Pointing her finger straight at the door, Tonya repeated the command. "Go!" Her bracelets jangled, and the candle's flame danced.

Betty grabbed her handbag and was out of the house faster than a horse running the Kentucky Derby.

Roscoe walked in from the kitchen. "Nice job, babe. You're getting really good at this."

"Did you take care of it?"

"Indeed." He held up his pocketknife. "That slow leak will be a flat tire by the time she hits her cozy little house in the suburbs."

"Nice."

Roscoe checked his watch again. "Rats! I need to change clothes and get over to the bank." He pulled at his tie and began unbuttoning his shirt. "You're going to have to handle things yourself until I get back."

"The bank? Why?"

"It's almost eleven. That McCarthy woman will be taking her smoke break soon. I have to get over there to be the 'dark, handsome stranger' you said she would meet." He gave her a wink as he strode to the bedroom.

"Just don't enjoy it too much," she called after him.

Tonya was the jealous type, no matter what the other woman looked like. Back in Las Vegas, Roscoe had a wandering eye. She was not about to let his eye or any other part of him wander off and leave her stranded and broke in the middle of nowhere. She was prepared to do whatever she had to in order to hold on to her man.

# Chapter 5

The cursor on Deena's keyboard blinked over and over as she tried to focus on her story. After talking to Lloyd and Laurie, she had lost her motivation to write. Opting to work at home, she had left the office with her head in a fog. Getting laid off would have been bad, but she was prepared to accept it. But writing features? That was another matter altogether.

Coffee might help. She got up from her desk and walked out of the formal dining room that she and Gary had converted into a home office.

Hurley followed her to the kitchen and sat by his dog bowl.

She gave him a sympathetic look. "No more food until dinner. The vet said you're getting too heavy."

The black terrier-mix tilted his head as if he didn't understand.

Deena knew he did. Ever since she'd gotten the pup from the animal shelter last fall, she had felt a connection. They could read each other's minds. She and Gary weren't able to have children, but she had definitely tapped into her mother's intuition when she adopted Hurley.

The coffee pot had cooled from the morning, so she poured what was left in a mug and put it into the microwave.

Out the kitchen window, she saw her neighbor, Christy Ann, loading two of her three children into their car seats. Must be time for Mommy's Day Out.

The microwave dinged, and Deena pulled out the hot brew, hoping a caffeine blast would motivate her literary muse.

She headed back to the office and set the mug on her desk. The clouds outside made the room darker than usual. She turned on the desk lamp and faced the screen again, determined to knock out the article. She hadn't missed a deadline yet, and she wasn't about to miss this one.

The new town slogan contest would be the story's lead. She flipped past the doodles in her notepad and found the details she needed.

As she typed, she spoke aloud. "The village idiots once again had nothing of importance to discuss. They came up with the lame idea to hold a contest to see who could piss the farthest. It was a draw." Luckily, the words on the screen didn't match her narration.

After muddling through her notes, she checked her word count. Close enough. Bert could pare it down to fit. She inserted the story into an email and hit "send." She'd wait a few minutes for a reply to make sure it was received.

She leaned her head back in the swivel chair and pictured the newsroom. Maybe she should have told Lloyd about her idea to follow up on Marty Fisk's re-zoning proposal. It could be her last chance at a real story before she started writing features about the Bluebonnet Club and spring gardening.

What if he weren't interested in the story and told her to drop it? She didn't want to risk it. With her mind made up, she decided to see what she could find out on her own before pitching it to Lloyd as a story. After all, the investigation—the thrill of the hunt—was the part of the job she liked best.

DINNER AT THEIR FAVORITE restaurant, Las Abuelas, was relaxing as usual. The aroma of roasted corn and spicy peppers provided the perfect pick-me-up. Gary suggested she have a margarita and offered to be the designated driver. Over dessert of warm sopapillas with honey, she finally got to the heart of the problem.

"You know, it's not that I hate feature stories, it's just not that challenging to me." She spread butter on the pastry. "I guess after spending all those years as a teacher, I was looking for something more." As she took a bite, honey dripped on the front of her blouse. She rolled her eyes and set the pastry back on her plate.

Gary snickered at her predictable mess. "I thought you wanted to work for the newspaper. That's all you talked about for the last two years before you retired—I mean, quit."

"See? I was afraid to say something because I thought you might say, 'I told you so.'" She dipped the cloth napkin in her water glass and dabbed at the spots on her blouse.

"It's not that, it's just that I'm worried you're looking for something that you won't be able to find." He wiped sugar and cinnamon off his mouth and took a drink of water. "This isn't some mid-life crisis, is it?"

The smirk on Deena's face answered that question. "I'm past mid-life by a mile. I guess I just thought working for the newspaper would be more rewarding. Truth. Justice. The American Way."

She took another bite and more honey fell to her lap. "I give up." She set the dessert back on her plate and dabbed her mouth with a napkin. "I thought I would be making a difference. Helping people."

"Like when you were teaching?"

"Yes, but..." She didn't know what to say, just like she couldn't put her finger on what was missing from her job. She sat back in her chair.

"What about that story you wrote on the school board banning water guns at the Halloween carnival? That started a protest movement."

"I wouldn't call a couple of teenagers carrying signs a movement. I don't know. I'll figure it out eventually."

Gary signed the check, and they headed outside. "Wait here. I'll get the car."

The skull and bones umbrella kept the rain off while she waited. With Gary's six-foot-two frame, they could never successfully coordinate sharing one umbrella. As he pulled up, she stepped across a large puddle and ducked into the car. "Do you mind if we take a detour on the way home?"

"No problem. Where to?"

"I want to drive over to the south part of town where Marty Fisk wants to re-zone. I'm curious about what's over there."

Gary pulled onto Main and headed south. "It's dark, so you won't be able to see much."

"That fine. I might be able to tell which of those old houses are occupied by the lights on inside."

"Good thinking, ace."

She stared out the window as the defroster cleared the windshield. They crossed over the railroad tracks. The shocks on Gary's red Mercedes were not as good as the ones on her SUV, and she jostled sideways. She was a little light-headed from the alcohol and wished she had skipped the margarita and ordered iced tea instead.

"Look. There's that new fortune telling business." Gary motioned over his left shoulder.

"I've heard about it. Sandra's been there."

"Figures."

Deena pictured Gary rolling his eyes even though she couldn't see them in the dark. Her husband was less understanding of Sandra's "quirks." He still agreed to occasional double dates because he liked Sandra's husband, Ian. They could talk about sports and politics and other things men talked about. Gary was an accountant; Ian was a lawyer. They shared some of the same clients.

Deena leaned forward and rubbed at the windshield. "Slow down. I think this is it."

The neighborhood consisted of three long streets with old houses. Some were vacant, others condemned.

As Gary drove down each street, she counted the houses that seemed occupied. "Not many people live here anymore. I counted nine houses that looked occupied."

A porch light came on next to them, and a gray-haired woman in a bathrobe stepped out her front door. She was holding a landline telephone with the receiver at her ear. She stared menacingly as they passed.

"Must be the neighborhood watch," Gary said. "Let's get out of here."

As they drove home, Deena wondered what it was about that specific area that made the councilman so interested. There were plenty of vacant commercial properties in the area. What was so special about those three streets? By the time she got home, her journalistic juices were flowing again, and her spirit was renewed.

First thing tomorrow, she planned to talk to Marty Fisk and to see what she could find out. Then she remembered her hair salon appointment. So that would be the second thing she'd do.

Curling up with Hurley on the couch, she made a list of questions to ask Fisk. She knew this might be her last news story, so she hoped it would be a juicy one.

# Chapter 6

A break in the clouds was a welcome sight for Deena as she headed downtown Wednesday morning. She lived in Butterfly Gardens, a suburban community on the west side of Maycroft. By the time she left the house, most of the neighbors were already at work, their kids dropped at school and the morning newspaper read.

Somehow, though, she always seemed to run into Christy Ann. After what she had done for Deena and her brother the previous December, Deena had tried to be extra nice to her. It wasn't always easy.

"Deena," Christy Ann called out in her best "yoo-hoo-neighbor" voice as she strolled up to the car.

Deena rolled down the window. "Hey, Christy Ann. I was just heading to the salon."

"Gotta get your roots done. I see that." She squished her face as though looking at road kill.

Deena forced a smile.

"I was just going to see if you wanted to buy some cookie dough from Charlie. It's a fundraiser for peewee soccer. You know, Charlie is on the all-star team."

"Is that so?" This was at least the fifth time Christy Ann had mentioned it. "Sure. Y'all stop by this evening, and I'll place an order."

"Great. I knew I could count on you." She smiled and blew an air kiss. "See you later. Oh, and you might want to have your lip waxed. I'm seeing that little mustache again."

Gritting her teeth, Deena returned the smile and closed her window. She white-knuckle drove all the way to town.

The Manely Beauty Salon was busy for a Wednesday morning. The break in the weather had sent everyone scrambling to make up for missed appointments. Deena waved to Kristy who still had another client in her chair.

"Be with you in a few minutes," Kristy called over the sound of chatter and blow dryers.

The magazine selection was slim, but Deena found a copy of *Southern Living* she had not yet read. As she sat in the waiting area, Charla, a real estate agent who lived two streets over, was talking to her hairdresser, Melissa.

Charla seemed even more animated than usual. "You wouldn't believe it! As I live and breathe, it was the craziest thing since Elvis Presley."

"Hold still now so I don't burn your ear." Melissa had the super-sized curling iron twisted around Charla's bleach-blonde locks.

Charla's voice grew louder. "The first time, she said I was going to have good fortune, 'cept she said it in this weird foreign accent. She must be from France or somewhere." She paused to blow on her freshly manicured nails.

Deena scooted to the end of the bench so she could hear better.

"I left there and headed to the Walmart. They were having a sale on beauty products, you know. Well, when I picked up my handbag out of the buggy, a twenty-dollar bill nearly bit my hand! I know it wasn't there before because I never carry cash. That-a-way, I can honestly tell any bums on the street that I don't have any money when they ask. I hate to lie, you know. It's not Christian."

"You can say that again." Melissa used a pick to fluff Charla's hairdo. She had to lower the chair to see the top.

"Is my hair too big?" Charla asked, squinting in the mirror.

"Why honey, there's no such thing!" Melissa opened the can of hairspray and took aim.

"Good. So, the next time I went, I—."

"I'm ready for you," Kristy said, interrupting Deena's gossip gathering.

She walked over to Kristy's station and took a seat, disappointed that she wouldn't get to hear the rest of Charla's story.

"Are we cutting today or just coloring?" Kristy re-arranged the utensils on her cart.

"Just color."

When Kristy walked to the back of the shop to mix up the dye, Deena strained to hear Charla. The shop was too noisy.

Kristy returned with the bowl of magic potion, guaranteed to turn Deena's gray roots to a shiny, medium brown. "I saw you listening to Charla. What was she jabbering on about?"

"I think she must have gone to that new psychic reader."

Kristy parted off a section of Deena's hair and began painting on the mixture. "She and half the town. Lots of my clients sit in this chair and tell me about going to 'Sister Natasha.'

That's what she calls herself. Some people have also seen a guy there. They say he's her brother."

Deena stared at Kristy in the mirror. "Have you been there?"

"No way. I'm not going to throw my money away on that bull malarkey. I've got mouths to feed." She reached for a towel and wiped away a drip on Deena's forehead.

"So what kind of things have people said about her?" Deena asked.

"That she tells their fortune. Sometimes it's good. Sometimes bad. It always seems to come true, though, just the way she says." Kristy shook her head. "Whatever. I'm not going to argue with a paying customer. I'm like a bartender. I'm paid to listen."

Deena smiled. "Once people get something in their minds, it's hard to reason with them."

"That's for sure."

Deena liked Kristy. She had a good head on her shoulders. They chatted amiably while Kristy finished applying the color and foil.

"Let me go wash this bowl out. I'll be right back." She walked toward the back of the shop.

"Mrs. Sharpe," someone whispered.

Deena spun around in the chair to see Cindy, the stylist next to Kristy, waving at her. "I heard what you two were talking about," she said in a low voice.

Deena wasn't the only one listening to gossip.

"I'll tell you this, ever since that psychic woman set up shop, there's been some strange things going on in Maycroft. Some people are really worried. There's been talk of evil spirits."

"Oh, good gravy!" Deena waved off the girl's words.

"*Shhh*. I'm serious. Just be careful. That's all I'm saying." Cindy turned back to her own client.

Deena's cell phone rang in her purse. The barking dog ringtone meant it was a call from someone other than Gary. She leaned down to see who the caller was before letting it go to voicemail.

Ian Davis. That's odd. Why would he be calling? She hadn't talked to Sandra's husband since December. She would call him back as soon as she left the salon.

All at once, Deena felt anxious to get the appointment over with so she could take care of business. She wanted to talk to Marty Fisk and perhaps some of the residents in that neighborhood. She needed to call Ian. And now, there was a new task to add to her list. Check out this fortune teller. She was curious to see what all the fuss was about.

# Chapter 7

**Eight hundred dollars** later, Roscoe's Toyota Corolla was held together on a wing and a prayer. The motor often backfired and the fumes from the tailpipe smelled of burnt rubber. He was not about to invest more money in a car when he was planning to abandon it once they crossed the border into Mexico.

He sat in the parking lot of the Central Savings Bank, peering out the foggy window. Almost time. Beverly McCarthy should be exiting the building any second. There she was.

One quick check in the mirror confirmed what he already knew. That slightly pudgy, thirty-something fool didn't stand a chance against his immeasurable charm. He had combed his hair to the side and dressed in khaki pants and a solid pink button-down shirt. Brown loafers completed the boy-next-door look he was going for.

He got out of the car and strolled in her direction where she had taken her usual spot on a concrete bench. He would have to be quick before her two friends from Accounts Payable showed up.

The woman looked up as he approached. His smile erased any fear she might have had in the presence of a total stranger.

"My angel. My darling. Can I trouble you for a smoke? My boss says I have to quit, but I'm finding it nearly impossible."

"Sure." She fumbled for the pack and offered it to him.

He drew out a cigarette and lit it with a flourish of match and flame. "Ahhh. That's heaven." He looked around. "What's a pretty lady like you doing sitting out here all alone? It's not safe."

She grinned, her face blushing. She tried to speak, but it came out as a jumble of sounds.

"I have a feeling you won't be alone long. Especially if I have anything to do with it." He took several more slow, sexy drags and blew the smoke up into the clouds. Then he looked at his watch. "Shoot. Got to get going." He winked. "See you again soon."

He walked back to his car just as her two companions were rounding the corner. As he reached for the door handle, he looked back over his shoulder to watch her excitedly relay the encounter to her friends.

"Hello, Roscoe."

He nearly leaped out of his loafer. "Jeez! You scared me."

"Get in. We need to talk."

"Now?" He looked around as though hoping someone might come to his rescue.

"Yes. You can talk to me or to the police."

Roscoe opened the door and got in. He really didn't have a choice.

# Chapter 8

A small town in Texas seemed like an unusual place for Ian Davis to live. He had gone to law school at Stanford in California and went straight to work for his father's firm. Corporate law held no interest for young Mr. Davis, so he soon left the firm for a job with Legal Aid. It paid the bills and kept him busy. Too busy for much of a social life.

A holiday trip to see his grandparents in Maycroft changed everything. That's when he met newly-divorced Sandra Berrie and fell in love with her big heart and playful spirit. When they talked of marriage, she dug her boot heels in and refused to leave her hometown. That's how Ian ended up working for the biggest little law firm in northeast Texas. The partners loved the fact that he was willing to handle the pro-bono cases they were required to take.

Before long, he and Sandra and three dogs and two cats had made a nice life for themselves.

When Deena left the salon, she sat in her car and returned Ian's call.

He answered on the first ring. "I'm glad you called. How have you been?"

"Fine." She knew he hadn't called to check on her health. "What is it, Ian? Is it Sandra?"

"Yes."

Deena gasped, alarmed something had happened to her friend.

"Don't worry. It's nothing bad. I'm just a little worried about her."

She let out her breath. "In what way?"

"I don't know if she told you, but we've been going to a fertility specialist in Dallas."

"I'm her best friend. Of course she told me." She shook her head. Men were so clueless.

"I don't know if it's the pills she's taking or what, but she's been acting really strange lately."

He must have noticed it, too. Deena hadn't thought about the pills and hormones being the problem. "I bet that's what it is, now that you say it. I'm actually relieved. I thought it might have something to do with her going to that new psychic."

"Psychic?"

She could hear the alarm in his voice. Hopefully, she hadn't given away a secret. "Um, didn't she tell you?"

"No. But I'm definitely going to talk to her about it. You know how superstitious she is already. She doesn't need some quack putting a bunch of mumbo jumbo in her head. Look, I need to go. Will you just keep an eye on her for me? Let me know if you notice anything wrong?"

"Will do." She assured him that he had nothing to worry about and that she would be in touch. But after hanging up, a feeling of dread washed over her. Not only was she concerned about Sandra's wellbeing, she was worried she might have broken a trust. Women don't tattle on their girlfriends.

But for now, she had bigger fish to fry. The pawn shop owned by Councilman Fisk was about ten minutes away. She wanted to get there before noon in case he might leave for lunch.

As she put her car in reverse, a strange man drove by in a paneled van. He wore sunglasses and a ball cap pulled down low on his face. It was much too overcast to be wearing dark glasses. He might as well have had a sign on the side of his vehicle that said, Creepy Stalker. She waited for him to pass and then pulled out to catch up with him. She scribbled his license plate number on her notepad, unsure if the second number was a three or an eight. Before she could get a good look at it, he turned the corner and sped off down Butler Road.

She continued toward the pawn shop. Surely, someone would report that vehicle to the police. There's usually at least one officer patrolling this area at all times. That thought made her check her speed. She tapped the brake pedal to slow down.

Several cars were parked in front of the pawn shop when she pulled up. Hopefully, Fisk would be there. She stepped around two riding lawn mowers on display in front of the door and walked in.

She had never been to a pawn shop before and expected it to be like the ones she saw on TV. The inside was bigger than she had imagined, rows of shelving filling much of the space. An attractive woman in her mid-forties sat on a stool behind a long glass case filled with handguns.

A young man held one of the pistols and examined it like a watchmaker valuing a fine timepiece. Another customer with a toddler in tow strolled down a row of small appliances. A door leading to an office area stood propped open. There was another salesman inside eating a sandwich and watching a small television. Fisk was nowhere in sight.

Deena walked to the counter and waited for the saleswoman to greet her. After waiting, she finally said, "Excuse me. I'm looking for Mr. Fisk. Is he here?"

The woman pushed her bright red hair back over her shoulder. "What do you want?"

Deena considered the question and the woman who asked it. By the looks of her low cut blouse, diamond bracelets, colorful tattoos, and bare ring finger, she wasn't the kind of person Deena wanted to tangle with. "I'm Deena Sharpe. I'm a reporter for the Tribune, and I wanted to ask him some questions about his re-zoning plan."

For some reason, the woman suddenly took interest in her. "It's about time someone paid attention to his plan. I'm Georgia Parks." She smiled and shot her hand out to shake. "Marty is usually here this time of day, but he left to run an errand. I'm not sure when he'll be back. I can call him if you want."

The man looking at firearms sneered at Deena. She had obviously interrupted the deal he was trying to make. She wondered if he were more interested in the gun or the girl. "I can come back later." She reached into her purse. "Here's my card. Just let him know I stopped by, will you?"

"You bet." She slipped the card into her bra and nodded her head.

Deena walked out the door and to her car. She reached for the seatbelt and stared down at her average-sized chest. She was glad Gary worked in an office where everyone was fully clothed.

Out of the corner of her eye, she saw someone drive past. Was it that same white van? Probably just her imagination. She pulled out of the parking lot and headed south toward the neighborhood she and Gary had driven through the night before. She wanted to talk to some of the residents to see what they knew about the re-zoning proposal. Maybe they had received offers on their property. Hard to believe anyone would be interested in the area for the houses themselves. As she got closer, she looked around, trying to determine why the area was of such interest to Fisk.

The first street was right off a small highway that headed south toward the interstate, the road most people in Maycroft took to Houston. Residents on that street were bound to hear a lot of traffic noise throughout the day and night. Deena turned onto the second street. She remembered seeing three houses in a row that seemed lit and occupied. She stopped in front of the middle one. It was as good a place to start as any.

The old wood-framed house likely had been built in the forties. It appeared to have had a second story added sometime later. Window boxes of petunias on the front gave it a well-kept look—compared to the surrounding homes, that is. She grabbed her tote and walked up the crumbling concrete path to the front porch.

She couldn't help but think about Scout in *To Kill a Mockingbird*. Scout had stood on Boo Radley's front porch and looked around the neighborhood in his shoes, through his eyes. She did the same thing on this stranger's front porch. What must it have been like to live here back in the day?

She snapped out of her daydream when she heard the faint sound of a television inside. The front window was raised, and she could see Dr. Phil's face on the screen. The doorbell button was missing, so she knocked on the screen door. It clamored back and forth as she struck it. She waited. Not hearing any footsteps, she knocked again. Harder.

Still nothing.

She peeked through the window and saw the top of a woman's head sticking up above the back of a rocking chair. Her gray hair was in a bun. She had probably fallen asleep watching TV. Or maybe she was hard of hearing. Deena called through the half-open window. "Hello?"

The woman didn't move, so Deena called again.

Nothing. She must be sleeping.

Deena turned to leave when something leaped off the chair, screeching and spitting. She stumbled backward as an orange cat jumped through the window and ran off the porch around the side of the house. With her hand on her chest, Deena tried to catch the breath that the scare had taken from her.

Surely, the woman couldn't still be asleep. Deena looked back through the window. This time, she saw the woman's pale arm swinging slowly over the side of the chair. Something was wrong.

She opened the screen door and turned the knob. It was unlocked. She crept toward the woman, each step creaking on the wooden floorboards. She moved around to the front of the chair and saw something she would not soon forget. The woman was dead. Strangled by a knitted scarf. The needles and ball of yarn lay resting in her lap.

The sound of someone screaming pulled out what little breath remained in Deena's lungs. She spun around toward the front door in time to see a woman fall faint onto the front porch.

GARY ARRIVED A FEW minutes after the police and ambulance. Deena was relieved to see him race up the front steps to where she was talking to Officer Cassidy Nelson of the Maycroft Police Department. Deena knew the female officer from their previous encounters.

"Are you okay?" He grabbed Deena and wrapped his arms around her.

"I'm fine." As soon as she said it, she felt her knees weaken. She leaned on Gary. "You remember Cassidy Nelson—I mean Officer Nelson."

"Of course." Gary reached out to shake her hand.

Deena looked over toward the front door. A paramedic attended to the elderly woman who had fainted. The medics had bandaged her head, but she was sitting up, yammering on about Barbara and crime and the city's neglect of its tax-paying citizens. She had identified herself as Millie Canfield, the next-door neighbor. Another police officer was taking her statement. Millie had apparently come out to check on Barbara Wilde—the victim—after she saw Deena pull up in her car and go to the door.

"Sorry about this, Mrs. Sharpe, but I just have a few more questions." Officer Nelson positioned herself between Deena and the front door.

"Certainly."

She looked back at her notepad. "You said you were here to interview some of the residents for the newspaper. Is that right?"

"Yes." Deena looked around as one of the paramedics came out of the house to go back to the ambulance.

"And if I check with Lloyd Pryor, he will verify that?"

Deena thought for a second. "Actually, no. I haven't told him about it. I thought I would talk to a few people first to see if there was even a story here." She squeezed Gary's arm tighter.

"Is that usual? To work on a story without talking to the editor?"

Deena's voice cracked as she spoke. "I—I don't know if it's usual or not."

"Hmm." Officer Nelson made a note.

Deena looked up at Gary, and then back at the officer. "Is there a problem?"

"I'm sure you realize we have to cover all our bases in a circumstance like this."

Deena suddenly felt as if she were a character in a movie. How could this be happening? She was the one who called 9-1-1. She had nothing to hide. Then she realized the circumstances sounded like the start of hundreds of police dramas.

A silver sedan pulled up in front of the house.

"Here comes Detective Evans. He'll be investigating the case, I'm sure. Just tell him what you told me, and you'll be fine." Officer Nelson took a few steps back. "Detective Evans, this is Deena Sharpe. She found the body."

He nodded. "Ma'am." He looked through the front door. "Would you give me a minute? I'd like to ask you a few questions before you leave. You can wait here, or Officer Nelson can take you down to the station where you might be more comfortable."

Deena looked up at Gary.

He put his arm around her. "Why don't we go to the station? There's no reason to stay here."

Deena nodded just as her cell phone barked loudly. It was Lloyd. She needed to talk to him about what was going on, but now was not a good time.

Officer Nelson closed her notepad. "I'll need you to ride with me in the squad car. You can follow us, Mr. Sharpe."

"Oh. Okay." He glanced at the street.

By this time, there were two police cruisers, the detective's unmarked car, a fire engine, and two ambulances parked in front. Deena's SUV was blocked in. Gary had parked farther down the street in front of the neighbor's house. He looked back at Deena. "We can come back to pick up your car later."

They waited as two paramedics lifted the gurney carrying the neighbor, Mrs. Canfield, down the front steps. As they wheeled her toward one of the ambulances, she let out another scream.

"That's it! That's it! Stop!"

The officer who had been questioning her ran down the steps. "What is it, ma'am?"

"That's the car I told you about! The one I saw last night." She pointed a crooked finger in the direction of Gary's red Mercedes.

"Are you sure?"

"Yes, yes. That's it!" She laid back and put her hands on her chest.

"Don't worry. We'll check it out." He nodded for the paramedics to take her to the ambulance.

Gary and Deena both stared toward the street, their mouths open.

"Is that your car?" Officer Nelson asked.

Gary nodded. "Yes. But I can explain."

"Okay, but let's wait until we get to the station." She motioned toward her vehicle. "I think both of you should ride with me."

Deena looked up at Gary. "Do we need a lawyer? Should I call Ian?"

"No," he said. "Everything is fine. For now."

As they followed Officer Nelson, an old Cadillac painted burnt orange and white with steer antlers tied to the front hood pulled up.

Deena recognized it. "You're kidding me."

Sure enough, it was Dan Carson, the Tribune's crime reporter who just got assigned Deena's political beat.

"Deena?" He seemed sincerely shocked to see her there. "You're not trying to steal my story, are you?"

She dropped her head and waited as Officer Nelson opened the back door of the squad car.

He shook his head and whistled. "I see. You're not stealing the story. You *are* the story."

AFTER TALKING TO HIS secretary to reschedule his afternoon appointments, there was little for Gary to do but wait. His interview with Detective Evans lasted less than ten minutes. Besides repeating several times why and when he and Deena had driven by the neighborhood the night before and what he knew about Deena's story, there was little else he could offer about the death of Mrs. Wilde.

It was all Gary could do to maintain his composure when the detective told him they were getting a warrant to impound his car for a few days to check it for evidence. Evans assured him it was for his own protection—to clear him from any wrongdoing.

Right. His car was his baby. It better not come back with scratches or that black powder they use for taking fingerprints. He might need Deena to pick up some more cloth diapers to use for polishing the exterior.

Deena.

As the clock ticked off the minutes, he fumbled through several magazines, not really even seeing the pages. All he could picture was Deena sitting across from Evans answering the same questions over and over. She was used to *asking* the questions, not answering them. Still, he knew she would be fine. She was innocent, after all.

The front door opened and Dan Carson sauntered into the station like he owned the place.

As a crime reporter, he probably hung out there. Gary had met him once when he and Deena were at a restaurant. He had been friendly enough, but Deena had been stand-offish. She said something about him bugged her. Gary wondered if maybe she were jealous of him and his accomplishments at the newspaper.

Carson walked over to the front desk and leaned on the counter to talk to the officer on duty. He must have said something funny or obscene or both because the woman cackled like a schoolgirl.

They talked a few minutes, and then Gary saw the officer motion in his direction.

Dan put his hand to his forehead and gave her a mock salute.

Gary remembered he had done the same thing at the restaurant. Must be his signature move. As Dan approached, Gary buried his nose deeper in the pages of *Sports Illustrated*.

Dan sat across from him and began talking as if they were old friends. "Crazy day. Am I right?"

Gary shrugged, not taking his eyes off the magazine.

"Deena is a real go-getter. Must be hard to keep up with her."

Gary glanced up and offered a half smile. He felt his jaw tighten. Maybe if he ignored this guy, he would just go away. The last thing he wanted was to have his name end up in the newspaper. He was determined not to take the bait.

Dan began humming softly to himself. The knot on his navy blue tie was loose. He undid the top button of his shirt, and kicked off some of the dried mud stuck to his Tony Lama boots.

Gary tried to ignore him. Obviously, the guy was plotting his next move. What was he going to try next? Chinese water torture?

Dan leaned forward. "So, does your wife often go around breaking into strangers' houses?"

That did it. Gary threw down the magazine. "Look Carson, you know darn well that she was working on a story. She's a reporter. She—" He was tempted to say more but caught himself.

"Easy, man. I hear you." He sat back and crossed his legs. "No need to go all Rambo on me."

Gary stood up and walked over to the front window. He jammed his hands in his pockets as he looked out into the parking lot. The clouds were merging again and threatening to spew. It had been almost an hour since he and Deena had gotten there. What could be taking so long?

A door opened near the front desk, and Deena emerged. She looked unshaken.

Detective Evans was behind her. "Wait here a minute, and I'll have an officer drive you home."

"Actually, I need to get my car."

He disappeared behind the door. Gary moved toward her. At least Carson had the decency to let him be the first to talk to his wife.

"I'm fine," she said, anticipating his question. She looked past Gary to Dan. "What are you doing here?"

"Hey, girl. I'm sure you know the routine," Dan said. "I wanted to see if I could ask you a few questions."

"You're kidding. No comment." She linked her arm through Gary's and took a defiant pose.

"C'mon. Throw a fellow reporter a bone. What were you doing at the old lady's house? Why did you break in?"

"I didn't break in. The door was unlocked."

Dan made a note on his pad. "You were worried about her, so you went in. You must have known the victim, right?"

"No. Yes—." She shook her head. "No, I didn't know her. Yes, I was concerned about her."

His eyes twinkled. "Why?"

Gary took a step forward. "That's all, pal. No more comments."

Dan smiled and closed his notepad. "I thought you were an accountant. You sound more like a lawyer." He raised his hand and saluted Deena. "See you back at the office." He waved toward the front desk and headed out the door.

"Thanks." Deena sat down and let out a deep sigh. "It's weird to be on the other side of things."

A young, fresh-faced deputy came around the corner. "Mr. and Mrs. Sharpe? I'll drive you home."

"We need to go back to...the scene," Gary said. "That's where her car is."

"You sure you want to go back there?"

The look of surprise on the officer's face was unnerving. Gary was ready to get out of there. "Yes, I'm sure."

As they exited the building, a flash of light caught them off guard.

"Sorry, Deena," the photographer said. "You know how it is."

Dan was leaning against his car and nodded as they passed by.

Gary walked faster and gnashed his teeth. "Since when is the hero of the story made out to be the bad guy?"

Deena ducked into the car. "In this business, it happens more than you think."

DESPITE THE DREARY drizzle, the entrance to Butterfly Gardens was a welcome sight. It seemed like days since Deena left to get her hair done this morning. She never would have dreamed it would have led to her being involved in another murder case. Maycroft was such a quiet place...usually.

Hurley jumped up and performed a circus-dog twirl when they came through the door. His excitement calmed Deena's nerves.

Gary opened the back door to let the dog outside. "You're going to call Lloyd Pryor first thing, right?"

"Absolutely. I just need to catch my breath a second." She hung her coat on the wall hook and dropped her keys on the entry table. Before she could even get to the bedroom, Lloyd was calling her on the phone again.

As she answered his questions and provided the missing details of the day's events, Deena could see Gary pacing the floor in the den. Hurley was back inside and right on his heels.

By the time she hung up, the knot in her stomach had started to unwind.

Gary walked into the bedroom, obviously worried about what would hit the morning newspaper. "What'd he say?"

She walked out to the den and sat on the couch. "Lloyd agreed not to run that picture of me in the newspaper. He also said Dan didn't write anything about me in his story except naming me as the person who found the body."

"That's a relief." Gary sat down in his leather recliner. "I was afraid Carson was going to make you out to be a suspect."

"I think he was just yanking your chain at the police station." She scratched Hurley's soft fur. "Lloyd did scold me for not telling him about the story before I started investigating. He wants me to tell Dan everything I know about Marty Fisk, which isn't much. Dan's going to follow up on it."

"Good. I'll feel better knowing you aren't any more involved than you already are." He turned on the TV and found a basketball game to watch.

"But it's my story," she whined.

Gary shot her a look of dismay. "Are you kidding me? That's what you're worried about? This situation doesn't just affect you. I have a reputation in this town. My job depends on people putting their trust in me."

She hadn't thought about that. Gary was her rock. Her Gibraltar. He was more dependable than a Maytag dryer. "You're right. Sorry."

He turned the sound back up on the game.

It was unusual for Gary to get upset with her. She didn't like it. Still, she wished she could help with the murder investigation for the newspaper. Until the police caught the killer—or at least had some other suspects—she was the only one under suspicion. And that was the last place she wanted to be.

# Chapter 9

"**Can you** let Hurley out?" Deena pulled the covers up under her chin. She waited, but the barking continued. When it finally stopped, she realized Gary wasn't even in the bedroom. She could hear the shower running, and Hurley was still curled up at her feet.

Finally she realized that the barking sound was the ringtone on her phone. She couldn't imagine who would be calling her this early in the morning. Prying one eye open, she picked up her phone and saw that the call had come from Sandra. She sat up and shook out the weeds growing in her head. Without even listening to the voicemail, she called back.

Sandra answered, not bothering with the usual niceties. "What on earth happened to you yesterday? I can't believe you didn't call me! Ian is furious with you."

"Good morning." Deena yawned and stretched like a house cat. "How did you find out?"

"It's in the newspaper. *Your* newspaper."

She'd forgotten about that. "By the time I got home, I was exhausted. Let me grab the newspaper so I can read the article." She put on her slippers and hurried to the front porch. A cold blast of air greeted her when she opened the door to pick up the paper. She quickly shut it and shuffled back to get under her warm blanket.

There it was on the front page. "Woman Found Murdered in South Maycroft Home."

"Deena? Deena!" Sandra yelled to get her attention.

"Sorry. I'm back." She skimmed through the article, spotting her name in the third paragraph. At least it wasn't in the lead.

"Here. Ian wants to talk to you."

"Deena? Why didn't you call me when all this went down? I'm your attorney."

She could hear genuine concern in his voice. "I didn't need a lawyer. I didn't do anything wrong."

"The story says you entered the house and found the body. Sounds to me like you did something. You're supposed to let me decide if it's wrong or not. Did they take you in for questioning?"

"Well, yes. Gary too."

"Gary? Why?"

She proceeded to explain some of the details, including the fact that Gary's car was impounded. As she relayed the events, she realized they sounded pretty bad.

Ian bombarded her with questions. Why didn't she tell her editor about the story? Why didn't she let the woman at the store call Marty Fisk? Why did she enter a private residence? These sounded like the same questions the detective asked her.

Ian used his stern lawyerly voice. "Promise me you won't talk to the police or the newspaper without calling me first. I'll see what I can find out from the police. Maybe they have some suspects."

She promised, and he seemed satisfied.

As she hung up the phone, Gary came in from the bathroom. "Who was that?"

"Ian. He's not happy with me—us, for not calling him yesterday. We are not supposed to talk to the police or anyone from the newspaper without calling him first."

"Sounds like good advice. I think you should lay low and stay home today. Besides, I have to take your car."

Deena folded her arms. "I forgot about that. I could drive you to work."

"Not a chance." He sat on the side of the bed to put on his socks.

"Great. It's like I'm in prison."

Gary spun his head around and stared.

"Oops. Hope I didn't jinx myself."

SPRING IS A TIME OF renewal. A time to refresh. But spring cleaning was of little interest to Deena as she stared at her closet. Without a car to go anywhere, she debated the need to even get dressed. She compromised by pulling on a pair of sweatpants and a t-shirt. Closing the door of the cluttered closet, she vowed to tackle it later. For now, she had a bigger job on her mind.

It had been ages since she had worked on restocking her booth at the Hidden Treasures Antique Mall. She occasionally stopped in for a quick dusting and visit with the owner, Janet. Being stuck in the house, she had no excuse to put the task off any longer. Like many resellers, she enjoyed buying more than selling and had accumulated a stockpile of goods to inventory, clean, and price.

Guided by a belly full of nervous energy, she opened the door to the guest bedroom where she kept all her purchases. Her reaction was mixed when she stared at the boxes, bags, and bundles she found inside. On the one hand, she dreaded the work ahead of her. But on the other, it was like shopping all over again as she spied some of the forgotten treasures.

Hurley brushed past her, anxious to explore all the new smells that waited for his curious nose.

"Let's get to it." She followed him in and pulled up an old wicker chair she had purchased in the fall. She picked up a box of breakables. American and English pottery were her specialty. Carefully, she pulled out several large vases and set them on an old card table.

The last entry in her inventory book was dated in December. That was after she and Sandra had gone to the flea market in Canton. She looked over on the shelf near the window. The sight of the two Southwestern vases made her shiver. It seemed like a lifetime ago that she had investigated Carolyn Fitzhugh's murder. She thought about her brother Russell and wished he'd return soon from Hawaii.

She recorded the amount she paid for the two pieces and removed their price tags. These two were clean inside so she didn't need to wash them. She grabbed a baby wipe that she used to remove surface dust and goo.

From experience, she had a good idea of the value of the vases. She filled in the inventory numbers and prices on her handmade tags and tied them on with raffia. Two down, a bunch to go. She really needed to do a better job of staying on top of this.

As she continued working, she thought about the previous day's events. What if she hadn't gone to Mrs. Wilde's house? What if she had gone to Millie Canfield's house instead? Mrs. Wilde might still be sitting in that chair waiting to be found. Bless her heart.

Deena believed that things tended to work out as they should. Maybe she was meant to show up there to find Mrs. Wilde. But the big question remained. Who would murder an old woman in her home? The story Dan wrote said the preliminary finding showed no evidence of a break in. They had contacted the victim's granddaughter who lived in town. She had verified that nothing appeared missing from the house.

The police would be looking at friends and family for a possible motive as was usual in this type of case. Maybe the woman had money. Greed is too often the motive for murder.

Was it a coincidence that the murdered woman lived in the exact neighborhood Marty Fisk wanted to re-zone? What was he going to do? Kill off the residents one by one? She shuddered at the thought.

A clap of thunder pulled her mind back before it had travelled too far down the road of suspicion.

As she looked around at the progress she had made, her thoughts turned to the piles of vintage items and who might have owned them before her. Had they been passed down from family members who had no interest in owning their relatives' old junk? After all, she did buy a lot of her inventory from estate sales. The sales were always a bit depressing, watching someone's memories redistributed piece by piece.

But like Gary always said about her business, it was the circle of life.

The doorbell rang and startled her and Hurley. He ran from the room barking. He might be small, but he was loud. He made a good watchdog.

Deena peeked through the hole, fully expecting to see her neighbor Christy Ann there to get the scoop on Maycroft's latest mystery. Instead, it was Dan Carson.

She opened the door and asked him in. "Where's your umbrella?" She took his wet jacket und hung it on the hall tree next to hers.

"Real men don't use umbrellas."

Deena rolled her eyes. "Whatever. Wipe your feet."

He stamped his boots on the mat and dried his wet hands on his jeans. Lloyd Pryor was an old-fashioned editor and required his male reporters to wear a tie. Dan's always seemed to hang loose around his collar. He followed her to the den. "Nice place."

"Thanks." She motioned to the sofa and sat down across from him. "I'm not supposed to talk to you about the murder case, you know."

"I figured. Pryor told me to get the information you have about Marty Fisk. That's the reason you were at that old lady's house, right?"

"Yep. I'll get my notes. Do you want some coffee?"

"Always." He pulled a pen out of his shirt pocket. "By the way, I know you didn't have anything to do with the murder."

Deena looked back over her shoulder. "Okay." Was she supposed to be relieved? She didn't need his absolution. She picked up her notebook from the desk and walked back to the kitchen to get two cups of coffee. When she walked back into the den, Dan was checking messages on his phone.

He took the cup. "So, what have you got?"

She flipped through her notes. "Marty Fisk has a plan to re-zone an area on the south side of town. He wants to make it commercial property. It's the neighborhood...I was in yesterday. He's made the proposal three times to the city council, and all three times it's been voted down."

"If the city re-zones, the few remaining residences would likely have to move." Dan scribbled some notes.

"I would assume so. Brad Thornhill is definitely against the plan."

Dan gulped the hot coffee like it were cool lemonade on a summer's day. "I don't know why he would be. That area is practically a wasteland anyway."

Deena looked up from her notes. "There are people who live there. People who have lived there their whole lives. You can't just run them off their property because you want to build a shopping mall or office complex."

Dan shrugged. "Seems like a conflict of interest if he's trying to use his position on the city council to his own benefit."

"That's what I thought, too." She picked up the cup and blew steam toward Dan. "I checked the records at the clerk's office and this is the only issue he has proposed since getting elected last May. Seems pretty determined."

"Has anyone voted with him?"

Deena flipped to another page. "In June, Councilman Dwyer did. Since then, he has voted against it."

Dan rubbed his chin. His scruffy beard showed the same hint of gray as his hair. "I'd be surprised if Fisk had the kind of money needed for that sort of development. I know he has some rental houses and owns the pawn shop, but developing a large property like that takes some major bucks."

"Maybe he has investors. Anyway, I was going to check with the residents to see if he had made them offers on their property or if they were aware of his plans." Deena took a sip of her hot coffee, wondering how Dan could withstand the heat.

"How badly do you think Fisk wants this re-zoning to happen?" He put his pen back in his pocket. "Bad enough to kill?"

"What?" Deena set her cup down and leaned in to see if he were serious. The playful twinkle in his eyes was missing. He wasn't kidding.

"Just thinking out loud. Don't tell me it hadn't crossed your mind?"

Of course it had. Deena stared back at her notes. She recalled how angry Fisk was when he stormed out of the meeting. She nodded slightly, not wanting to commit to an answer.

"Is there anything else?" He thumbed the pages of his notepad.

"There's a woman at the pawn shop. Georgia Parks. She seems more than casually interested in Fisk's plans."

"I'll talk to her." He stood up. "Thanks for the coffee."

Deena stood up and walked toward the front door. "Will you let me know if you find anything out?"

"About Fisk?"

"And the murder."

He flicked her a salute. "See? Even you think they're connected."

# Chapter 10

Roscoe fidgeted with his hair. He'd been wearing it slicked down so often lately that it didn't want to go back to its usual style.

Tonya walked into the kitchen where he was drinking a beer. "What did you do? It reeks of cologne in here?"

"I was trying to cover up the mildew smell." He picked up the saucepan from the floor and emptied out the rainwater. Luckily, the shingles on the roof had swelled enough to quell the leak to a slow drip.

"I thought you were going to get that fixed?" Tonya pulled the belt of her robe tighter around her waist.

"It'll happen. They can't repair it until it stops raining and dries out." He didn't want to tell her he hadn't had the nerve to ask Marty Fisk to repair it.

"Where are you going?"

"Out."

"Out where?"

"To the market." He stood up and walked over to the kitchen window. It was almost dark.

"You went to the market yesterday." Tonya took a drink out of his bottle.

"I forgot some things." He kept his back to her.

"Okay, but just be sure to get some more candles. And some matches. I'm going to lay in bed and watch a movie." She got up and put her hand on his back. "See you when you get back. Hope I'm not asleep."

He leaned down to kiss her. "Me, too."

As she walked off down the hall, he let out a sigh of relief. Hopefully, this wouldn't take long. He pulled out a photograph from his pocket and stared at it again. After studying the face for a minute, he put the picture back in his pocket and zipped up the front of his jacket.

The front door creaked as he opened it, reminding him of a haunted house in an old Vincent Price movie. He jumped off the front porch onto the gravel drive, avoiding the muddy yard. He got in his car and headed south.

The Hitchin' Post Saloon was just a few blocks away. He pulled into a back parking spot. Thursdays were Ladies' Night, and judging by the cars, there was a good-sized crowd inside. That would help him blend in. He waited for another car to pull up and then followed two men with cowboy hats through the front door. He quickly cased the room and headed for a table occupied by two thirty-something women.

Just as he thought, they were more than happy to let him join them. He signaled for a waitress. She was a blond. Not the girl he was looking for. He ordered a Bud Light. Usually, he only drank imported beer, but he didn't want to draw attention to himself.

"Where are you from?" one of the women asked. She flipped her red hair back off her shoulder, revealing a tattoo of a snake crawling through a heart.

"Dallas. I'm on my way to Houston and just stopped in for a beer. I didn't know Mayberry had such pretty women."

"It's Maycroft, silly, not Mayberry!" The other woman put her hand on his leg and gave it a squeeze. The white fringe hanging from her red rodeo shirt reminded him of the girls in Vegas.

"Aw shucks. I forgot."

Tattoo woman giggled and pulled at her neckline, revealing ample cleavage. Fringe woman sneered at her.

Last thing he needed was a catfight. "Can I get you two another beer?"

"Sure, honey." Fringe girl let her hand slide up his leg as he stood.

He winked. "Now don't you go lettin' no snake charmer take my seat while I'm gone."

They both giggled this time, and he escaped toward the bar. Another waitress was carrying six beer bottles to a table near the dance floor. She had brown hair but didn't look like the girl in the photograph.

Then he spotted her. She was behind the bar pulling draft beer from taps. Even with the melancholy look on her face, she was a beauty. He nudged his way forward until his arm rested on the well-worn, wooden ledge.

"What can I do ya?" she asked without making eye contact. She seemed intent on wiping down the counter in front of her.

"What do you recommend?"

Her blue eyes flashed annoyance in his direction. "Recommend? It's a bar. You order beer."

"Then I'll have a beer." He smiled and looked at her anxiously, hoping she'd smile back.

She grabbed a glass mug and yanked on the tap, filling it until foam covered the top. "Here!" She slammed it onto the counter and defiantly crossed her arms.

"This guy ain't giving you trouble, is he?" A surly man working the other end of the bar stared him down.

"Not yet." She grabbed the dish towel and started wiping up the mess she'd made.

Roscoe pulled out a twenty-dollar bill and slid it her direction. "Keep it." He took a sip and pulled the glass away to reveal a foam mustache. "Is something wrong?"

The girl looked at him and chuckled. "Don't make me laugh. My heart is broken."

A broken heart? That reminded him of Tattoo and Fringe. He glanced back over his shoulder and lifted up on his toes. Luckily, they had found two other unlucky suckers to join them. He was off the hook.

He watched as the girl at the bar with the soft brown hair and glittery blue eyes served several other men who occupied barstools. He fished for just the right words. He needed to sound caring.

"I'm sorry about your heart. Anything I can do to help?"

"Not unless you can bring my grandmother back. She died yesterday. In fact, she was murdered."

"Murdered?" He spit foam down the front of his shirt. That son-of-a-gun hadn't told him she was murdered. What had he gotten himself into? He took another drink and tried to appear relaxed.

The girl looked as though she would burst into tears.

"I'm really sorry. What are you going to do with her house...and stuff?" That sounded so lame. What a stupid question. He must be losing his touch.

As though having a conversation with herself, she began talking. "I don't know what I'm going to do. Her funeral mass is tomorrow. I used to live with her until I saved up for my own apartment. I could move back in, but that would be creepy. To live where she was killed. It's full of so many memories. But it's paid for and part of the family. Then there's my brother. He—"

She must have realized she was spilling her guts to a complete stranger. She stopped, and her ivory cheeks flushed to a soft pink.

He smiled. "It's fine. I'm sure things will work out."

Nodding, she took another order.

As much as he wanted to stay—to take her in his arms and comfort her—he knew he needed to leave. Tonya would be suspicious. He chugged the rest of his beer and made his way to the door. Looking back over his shoulder, he made a promise to himself. If things didn't work out with Tonya, he would be going to Mexico without her.

Instead, he would be taking Katy Wilde.

# Chapter 11

Gary was like a bull in a china shop when it came to Deena's antique booth. She only trusted him to load boxes of collectibles into her car with her walking right next to him, reminding him to set them down gently. She had filled eight boxes to take to the booth.

Luckily, Gary had gotten a ride to work from a co-worker who also lived in Butterfly Gardens, telling him his car was in the shop. It wasn't exactly a lie. There was probably a shop at the police station where they dusted for fingerprints and searched for hair and blood evidence. Her husband kept his car immaculate, unlike Deena, so they probably wouldn't need as long to examine it.

Before going to her booth, she needed to stop by the thrift shop to talk to Sandra. Besides checking up on her for Ian, she wanted to talk to her about the murder and Marty Fisk.

Three cars were parked in front of the shop when she pulled into the parking lot. The promise of sun and heat had brought people back out of their houses that bright Friday morning. The streets, grass, and trees all glistened from their overnight bath. The weatherman predicted sunshine at least through the weekend. He was an optimist.

Sandra was laughing with a customer who was trying on vintage hats. It was good to hear her laugh. Maybe she was in better spirits.

"Hey there. Glad you stopped by." Sandra glanced around to see if anyone needed her help, then motioned for Deena to follow her to the storeroom. Sandra's eyes widened. "When you left here Wednesday, I thought you were going to the pawn shop. What happened?"

"I did. Fisk wasn't there, so I drove over to the neighborhood."

"I'm so glad you're okay, but I can't believe there's a killer running loose in Maycroft. Wait here." Sandra went to the counter to check out several customers.

Deena looked around. Boxes of merchandise that had recently come in sat near the back door. Deena rifled through to see if there was anything interesting. She was disappointed to find they were mostly worn-out clothes.

Sandra returned for coffee. "You know what you should do? You should go see Sister Natasha. She might be able to tell you who the killer is."

Deena put both hands to her cheeks. "Seriously? You don't believe that, do you?"

Sandra dropped her shoulders. "How can you be such a naysayer when you haven't even gone? You should at least go one time before you make up your stubborn, closed mind."

"Maybe you're right." She didn't want to ruffle her friend's feathers. "As a matter of fact, I'm planning to write a feature story on her. Maybe we should go together."

A frown crept across Sandra's face. "I'd be surprised if she talks to you. People like her don't really like to talk about their gifts."

Gifts. Deena tried to sound sincere. "What exactly does she do? Does she have a crystal ball? Does she read your palm?"

Sandra's eyes lit back up. "No. It's really interesting what she does. Instead of tarot cards, she has a deck of regular playing cards. She asks you to shuffle, and then she places two cards down in front of you and turns three over in the middle of the table. She studies those for a minute. Then she places another one up, then another one. Finally, she turns over your two cards and has an epiphany. That's when she tells you your fortune."

Deena stared. She pictured the scenario as Sandra described it. Her mouth dropped open. "That's not fortune telling. That's Texas Hold 'Em!"

"What? No." Sandra shook her head. "You—"

Sandra's cell phone rang and interrupted her protests. Her eyes widened as she spoke to the caller. "What? Who? We'll be right there." She ended the call. "Let me get my purse! We've got to go!" She ran off to the storeroom.

"Why? What's happened?" A knot the size of Texas twisted in Deena's gut.

"The Coleman boy, Brandon. He's gone missing down by the river. They're calling people to help search. We'll take my car."

Deena's legs suddenly felt full of lead. Bile burned her throat. It was all she could do to make it to the car. The thought of a missing child was almost too much to bear. She had known the Colemans for years. She managed to get to the car and buckle up.

Sandra raced down Main. Sirens blared in every direction.

Deena's head began to clear as they bounced across the railroad tracks. Then it hit her. Something was not right. "Where are you going? This isn't the way to the river."

"We're not going to the river."

TONYA PACED THE FLOOR. She had pretended to be asleep when Roscoe rolled into bed last night, smelling like he'd bathed in cheap beer. When she woke up to discover he hadn't bought the candles and matches—or anything for that matter—she went ballistic.

He brushed off her anger, slamming the door behind him as he left to go back to the market.

At least she hoped that was where he was going. She already had three appointments this afternoon, and they usually saw a handful of walk-ins. Trying to concentrate on getting her make-up properly applied was next to impossible with her hands shaking with rage.

Here she was, stuck in Texas with a guy on the run and no money. But that wasn't the worst of it. She was crazy about Roscoe. Besides his good looks and boyish charm, he made her feel safe. At least he used to. If he left her...

No. She couldn't let that happen. The mascara wand slipped from her fingers and brushed across her cheek on its way to the sink.

Someone banged on the front door, much louder than usual. She heard the door open and someone calling out. Darn that Roscoe! He must have forgotten to lock it behind him. She wiped at her cheek and grabbed her shawl. She looked at the turban, but there was no time to put it on. The last thing she wanted now was for a customer to pull back the curtain.

"Wait! Wait!" She forgot about her accent. Luckily, no one was in the kitchen when she got there. Taking a deep breath, she slipped through the curtain into the parlor. Surprised, she saw one of her best customers, Sandra Davis.

"Sister Natasha. Thank goodness you're here. I need you to come with me."

Tonya took a step back. "Come? Where?"

Sandra's words came in short breaths. "To the river. There's a child missing. You have to help find him."

"Natasha no come. No leave house." She shook her head and walked toward the table.

Sandra caught her by the arm. The look on her face was a mixture of terror and desperation. "Natasha. We need your help. You can do this. I know it."

Taken off guard by the woman's pleas, she nodded her head and followed Sandra to the door.

When they got out to the car, Tonya squinted against the bright sun. It had been days since she'd been outside.

Another woman got out of the passenger's seat and into the back of the car.

Tonya got in and tried to steady her hands as she fastened her seatbelt. What was she doing? She wasn't a psychic; she was a fraud.

"Sister Natasha, this is my friend, Deena." Sandra pulled out and sped off toward the river. "What kind of information do you need? The boy's name? An article of his clothes?"

Tonya's mind was a blur. She knew she had seen this kind of search on TV or maybe in a movie. "Name."

"Brandon Coleman. He's about four years old. His mother was shopping at Creekside Village. Have you been there?"

Tonya shook her head. "No." That was the first honest thing she had said in a long while.

"There are stores and restaurants all along there. And walkways leading down to the river. But with all this rain, the water level is up. He might have..."

Tonya closed her eyes. This was serious stuff, not the pranks she and Roscoe usually played. Sure, they would put money in a woman's purse or take some out. Once, they put in a small mouse they had caught under the kitchen sink. Occasionally, Roscoe would show up at someone's house or office in disguise. It was easy to find their addresses when he slipped their wallets out of their purses. He sometimes went online to find information. People were such suckers.

But this was different. Her chest tightened as she tried to stop the flood of memories crashing through her head. Michael...her step-brother...just disappeared. Her hands flew up to her face as she yelled. "Stop!"

"What is it?" Sandra turned wide-eyed toward Tonya and pressed the brake. "Do you see something?"

She hadn't realized she'd screamed. "No. Drive."

Sandra parked behind a pack of cars jammed behind the Rounder's Café. Scores of people were combing the water's edge and calling out for the boy.

They got out of the car. Deena headed down toward the water.

Tonya surveyed the scene, holding back tears. For a moment, she didn't know if she were crying for Brandon or Michael. She couldn't do this. Not when there was a life involved.

Sandra took her by the arm, more gently this time, and walked her behind the café where they had a clearer view of the water. She let go of Tonya's arm and took a step back.

Tonya closed her eyes. *Lord, help me find this child.* It was the first time she had prayed in years. She clenched her hands together and took a deep breath. As she let it out, a strange taste seemed to fill her mouth. It was sweet. What was it exactly? Cherry? Bubble gum? "Candy." The word slipped out of her mouth.

Sandra stepped in closer. "Did you say 'candy'?"

"Yes. Candy."

"Are you saying you want some candy?"

"No." Tonya opened her eyes and looked straight at Sandra. "I taste candy."

Sandra's brows furrowed. Then she blinked several times and her mouth gaped. There's a candy store down the way. "Do you think Brandon's there?"

"I don't know." She didn't even bother to use her accent.

"Let's go check." Sandra headed back to her car.

Tonya got in. Her mind seemed blank. She had no thoughts about whether they were on a wild goose chase. All she could think about was the sweet taste of candy overwhelming her senses.

They drove several blocks and pulled in front of Sally's Sweet Treats. The building was old. Like many of the storefronts, this one had originally been built as a residence back before the area was zoned for commercial use.

Sandra opened the building's front door. The place was empty. "Brandon!" she yelled over and over.

They headed to the back storeroom. Nothing.

Tonya's stomach began to churn, and she felt nauseous.

Sandra opened a door leading out the back of the store. They walked down four steps to the muddy grass behind the building.

A banging noise caught their attention. They heard a small cry like a cat's wail. On the far side of the building was another door. Sandra bounded up the steps and yanked it open. There, in a ball on the floor of an old mudroom, was little Brandon Coleman.

Sandra scooped him up, tears flowing down her cheeks as she carried him outside.

Tonya stood in stunned silence. She blinked her eyes. She couldn't believe it.

"He's here!" Sandra yelled.

It didn't take long for a tearful crowd to gather around them.

Pushing her way through was a woman who could only be Brandon's mother. She sat in the wet sod, rocking her son and crying. The little boy squirmed, but she held him tight.

Tonya suddenly felt very exposed. Her long heavy skirt and shawl made her stand out like Rudolph's red nose. She lowered her head and inched through the crowd toward Sandra's car. Word of her involvement spread quickly. Just as she got into the backseat and shut the door, a wave of people came splashing toward her. She covered her face with her shawl.

Onlookers were taking her picture with their cell phones. A police officer stretched out his arms to hold back the throng. A photographer's rapid-fire flash was like lightning striking right in her face. Deena was talking to a man taking notes. Sandra was talking to another police officer. The squeal of the sirens seemed deafening now.

Tonya lowered her head and squeezed her eyes shut. She was used to being gawked at on the stages of Las Vegas, but this was different. She felt like a sideshow freak. All she wanted was to get back to the safety of her little house.

Sandra and Deena got in the car, and they drove away slowly. No one spoke. They must have sensed her anxiety. When they pulled up in front of Tonya's house, she was relieved to see Roscoe's car parked in front.

He came out of the house and rushed up to retrieve her. "Where have you been?" He was dressed in his street clothes and spoke without an accent.

Sandra stood by her car door. "Be gentle with her. She's had a big day."

As they hurried to the house, Roscoe looked back over his shoulder. "What do you mean?"

"She's a hero."

"SPILL IT," ROSCOE DEMANDED. "What did you do?"

Tonya was emotionally spent. Her head hurt and her stomach churned. Was Roscoe going to be mad at her? It's not like she had a choice. They practically dragged her out of the house. Slowly, methodically, she relayed the morning's events.

Roscoe found the whole thing amusing. "A hero? That's a laugh. If you're a hero, I'm the Pope!"

Relief washed over her as she realized he wasn't angry.

In fact, he was practically giddy. "I don't know how you did it, but this might be the greatest con of all! Imagine the publicity we'll get. The money we'll make. You're a genius." He leaned over and kissed her cheek.

Tonya shook her head. "But that's just it. It wasn't a con. It really happened."

"Yeah, whatever."

"No, I'm serious. I think I might be psychic. For real."

Roscoe snickered. "Get out of here. Don't be stupid."

"Well, how else would you explain it?"

"A lucky guess. It's not that far-fetched to think a kid might go to a candy store. Now stop this nonsense. We have to start making plans for the customers who are going to come knocking down our door."

The sound of cars pulling up outside drew him to the window. "Bingo. Here they come. Get in there and fix yourself up. Don't forget your turban." He raced to the kitchen to get the new candles to set out in the parlor.

"I can't!" she cried and sniffed back her tears. "Not yet, at least."

Roscoe's eyes blazed, but then a smile crept across on his face. "You're right. Good thinking. Always leave them asking for more. He grabbed his jacket from the hall tree and pulled the mustache out of his pocket. Patting down his hair, he turned to her. "Go to the back of the house. I'll take care of this."

Relieved, she slipped behind the curtain and listened as Roscoe performed his magic.

He opened the door and began speaking like the town crier, but with a foreign accent. "Good people of Maycroft. Sister Natasha wishes to be alone. Today, no visitors. Come back tomorrow."

He closed the door. His sinister laughter filled the room.

She hurried to the bedroom and began to un-Natasha herself. A hot bath might make her feel better. For the first time, she locked the door behind her. A generous amount of bubble bath turned into an ocean of fluffy clouds. She immersed herself in the hot foam, her eyes closed, cheeks flushed.

The sweet smell of jasmine filled her nostrils and took her back in time. Back to her childhood and that small Arkansas town. All she could think about was her stepbrother's disappearance. Always in the back of her mind, today's ordeal had moved it front and center.

She was supposed to be watching him, but she was too busy talking to a friend on the phone. She was fifteen; Michael was seven. She hadn't heard the car. Or the door open. Or Michael cry out to her. One minute he was there; the next minute he was gone.

The police investigation turned up few leads. They concluded that her stepfather probably took him to Mexico.

She slipped down beneath the bath water until she was completely submerged. If only *she* could disappear.

AS THEY DROVE BACK to the shop, Deena was at a loss for words. Several times she started to speak, but the words stuck in her throat. Had she just witnessed magic or a miracle? She couldn't wrap her mind around it.

She felt the same way two years ago when she and Gary had gone to Las Vegas and watched a performance by the great magician David Copperfield. She knew what she was seeing was a trick, but she just couldn't figure out how it worked. Maybe this "Sister Natasha" was the real deal. A woman with a God-given gift to see what others couldn't. To know things others didn't know.

Sandra pulled up next to Deena's car at the thrift shop and turned to her non-believing friend. "So, what do you think now?" Her Cheshire cat grin taunted Deena.

"I guess you were right." Deena opened the car door and got out. "I never would have believed it if I hadn't been there myself."

Sandra shook her head. She walked over and gave Deena a big hug. "Go home. It's been a crazy day."

The boxes of inventory piled on the seats and in the cargo area of her SUV suddenly seemed insignificant. She'd wait and take them to her booth tomorrow. "I think I will."

She got in her car and waved to Sandra as she started for home. She couldn't wait to tell Gary what had happened. As she approached Butterfly Gardens, one thought kept circulating through her mind. This was gonna make one heck of a feature story.

# Chapter 12

When a person is found murdered with no obvious motive, the first place police go looking is into the victim's family. In this case, that meant Barbara Wilde's grandchildren—Katy and Travis. Their parents had died in a car accident ten years earlier. They had moved in with their grandmother who took care of them until they could fend for themselves.

The coroner determined that Mrs. Wilde took her last breath sometime between eight o'clock and midnight on Tuesday evening.

Katy Wilde had a rock solid alibi. She was working her shift at the Hitchin' Post Saloon until two in the morning. Witnesses verified her story. The other bartender had called in sick. She barely had time for a pee break, much less for sneaking out, strangling grandma, and sneaking back in without being missed.

Witnesses also described Katy as wholly devoted to her grandmother who had helped support her emotionally and financially. With Katy having no opportunity and no clear motive, the police moved on to her brother Travis. The problem was that he seemed to have disappeared.

These were the facts as Dan Carson knew them when he entered the Lucky Strike Pawn Shop late Friday afternoon. He had already filed his story about the rescue of the missing boy. As it turned out, there wasn't much to write. Someone else would have to follow up with a feature story on the psychic.

But now, he was following his reporter's nose for news.

The place was busy with customers who had brought in anything they could get their hands on to pawn for a little extra weekend spending money. Marty Fisk was behind the counter brokering a deal on a set of golf clubs.

Dan recognized several of the employees, including Georgia Parks, a woman he had known since high school.

Georgia stood behind the counter, smoothing back her fiery red hair and crossing her arms. "Well, Dan Carson. As I live and breathe. I never expected to see you here in our fine establishment."

Dan reached in his pocket and offered her his handkerchief. "Here. Use this to wipe that sarcasm dripping out of your mouth."

She rolled her eyes and walked up to a man who was looking at gold watches in the glass case. Without turning her head, she asked, "What are you doing here anyway? Shopping, I hope."

"No chance. I'm here to talk to your boss." He pulled out his notepad.

She looked up. "About what?"

Dan snickered. "You'll find out when you read it in the paper. You do read, don't you?"

Georgia mouthed something obscene.

The man looking at watches turned around and glared at Dan like a would-be assassin.

Dan put his hands up in the air and took a few steps back. Last thing he needed was a scuffle. "Whoa, buddy. We're old friends, she and I. Save your chivalry for someone who deserves it."

When Dan turned around, he walked smack into a guy imitating a brick wall.

"Can I help you?" the man asked. He stood between Dan and the front door.

"I'm here to talk to Councilman Fisk."

The hulk turned his head and whistled. "Hey Marty, this weasel needs to talk to you."

Fisk nodded and walked toward the office.

"Thank you for your help. And keep your eye on her," Dan said, pointing to Georgia. "She can't be trusted."

As Dan headed toward the office where Fisk was waiting, he tried to recall the root of the animosity between himself and Georgia. As best he remembered, it had something to do with a high school football game and his getting caught kissing her younger sister behind the bleachers.

"Dan Carson," he said when he entered the office, sticking out his hand congenially.

"Yes. I know who you are." Fisk returned the handshake. "Sit down. Are you here to ask about my re-zoning proposal? What happened to that other woman who was here the other day? He moved around the papers covering his desk, and then yelled into the store. "Hey Georgia? What did you do with that reporter's card?"

She walked in and pulled open his top desk drawer.

He reached in and got it. "Oh, here it is. Deena Sharpe."

Georgia slammed the drawer shut and walked over to the doorway. She leaned on it like a character out of a Tennessee Williams play, looking sultry and foreboding.

Dan snickered then turned back to Fisk. "Deena's not on the story anymore. I am."

"That's fine. So what do you want to know? I have a report here...somewhere..." He shuffled more papers. "...detailing benefits to the city."

Dan waved his hand. "Don't bother. I just want to ask you a few questions."

Fisk leaned back in his chair. "Okay, then. Shoot."

"So, you were pretty heated when you left Tuesday's Council meeting, from what I hear."

"Yes sir. That bunch down there is dumber than a blond girl in beauty school. Ain't none of them have any idea how to make money—for the city, that is."

Dan nodded his head. "Politics. Am I right? Whatcha gonna do."

"If they would just re-zone that neighborhood on the south side—"

"The one where Mrs. Wilde was found murdered on Wednesday."

Fisk raised an eyebrow. "Yeah, that one...then they could tear down those shacks and build an office complex or a factory or a shopping mall."

Georgia was still standing in the doorway. She winked at Marty.

Dan tapped the notepad on his knee. "Those 'shacks' as you so kindly refer to them, are people's homes. What's going to happen to them?"

"Maybe you've heard of a little thing called 'eminent domain.' Sacrifice a few for the good of the rest."

"And by the 'rest,' do you mean yourself? Are you planning on buying up that property for yourself?"

Fisk sat up straight in his chair. "Is that any of your business?"

"It's the city's business if a councilman has a conflict of interest." The tension in the room was thicker than quicksand.

Marty took a deep breath, his eyes blazed. "If you're implying—"

"I'm not implying anything, Marty. Calm down." Dan shuffled in his chair. "Let's get back to Tuesday's meeting. You left mad that they wouldn't approve your proposal, is that right?"

Marty unclenched his teeth. "Yes." He glanced at Georgia.

"So where were you around ten o'clock on Tuesday night?"

Fisk slammed his fist on the desk. "What are you, a reporter or a cop?"

"I'm just asking questions. Don't get excited. I assume you were in bed sleeping." Dan nodded toward the picture on the wall of Fisk with his wife and two kids.

"That's right." He practically growled the response.

Dan tossed a glance at Georgia, and then asked, "With whom?"

Fisk jumped from his chair. "Get out! Get out of here! I'm calling your boss! Somebody get me that man on the phone!"

Dan didn't hesitate as he hurried to the front door. He turned around to wave a salute to Georgia just as the hulk came charging toward him. He was out the door and into his Cadillac faster than a jackrabbit on speed. "You may be fast, but us weasels are faster," he called out.

As he drove away, he felt a mixture of elation and regret. He needed more information before he went to the cops. Fisk and Georgia would never agree to talk to him again after what just happened. Right now, all he had was his gut. But if his instincts were right, he may have just found a killer.

# Chapter 13

"**C'mon, Dan,**" Deena said as she checked her watch. Any more coffee and she was going to turn brown. She stared out the window of the Highway Café. It was Saturday, and she needed to get her merchandise on the shelves of her antique booth.

An elderly couple sat next to each other in a booth across the way. The woman cut her husband's biscuit in half and smeared it with strawberry jam. Deena smiled, thinking how that could be her and Gary someday.

The waitress leaned against the counter with her hand on the coffee pitcher, ready to swoop in with a refill. She chatted pleasantly with a cook.

Deena picked up the spoon and rubbed it clean with her napkin. She tried to see her face, but it was upside down. She picked up the knife.

The door swung open, and Dan trudged in, stopping to wipe his feet. "Clara, fix me up with some coffee, would you, cutie?"

She patted the side of her silver body-wave and had his cup filled even before he sat down. "What'll you have today, handsome?"

"Just coffee, for now. Check back in couple of minutes." He waited for Clara to walk away before apologizing to Deena. "Sorry I'm late." He laid his jacket over the back of the booth. "I was at the police station."

She was all ears. "So, what's up? And why did you want to meet outside of town?"

"Because...I didn't know if you wanted to be seen with me."

Deena's squinted her eyes. "Umm, is there something I'm missing?"

He tossed back his head. "Nah. Nothing like that. It's about Fisk and the dead woman."

"That's what I assumed. Have you found out anything new?" She leaned in as though they were sharing confidential military secrets.

"The cops cleared the granddaughter, Katy. Now they're looking for her brother. Word is there might be a fairly sizable insurance policy out there." He motioned to Clara. "Can I get a club sandwich here please?" He turned back to Deena. "You want anything?"

"I'll have the same."

Clara nodded and headed into the kitchen.

Deena pulled paper napkins out of the metal holder on the table. "Have Gary and I been cleared?" She handed a stack to Dan.

"No one has come out and said it, but it's pretty obvious you two weren't involved. Did Gary get his car back?"

"Yesterday."

"My guy down there did say that your husband's car was the cleanest one they'd ever seen. Almost too clean."

"That's Gary. He loves his little baby."

Dan gulped down his coffee. "Like me and my Caddy. But mine's a pig sty."

She lowered her voice again. "So has anybody mentioned Marty Fisk?"

"Not a word."

"What are you going to do?"

Clara brought the sandwiches and refilled their cups.

Dan gave her a wink and waited until she returned to the kitchen. "I paid a visit to the pawn shop yesterday. I wanted to feel him out. Came away with two thoughts." He took a big bite of his sandwich and reached for a napkin to wipe mayonnaise off his chin.

His words hung in the air like yesterday's laundry. She couldn't stand it. "What? Tell me."

He glanced to the side. "Marty Fisk is up to something. He wants that property for himself. I don't know what he's planning to do with it, but it sure isn't about helping the city."

That confirmed Deena's suspicions as well. "What else? You said you had two thoughts."

"He's having an affair with Georgia Parks?"

"Really? How do you know?" She chomped on a few potato chips while she waited.

He laid down the sandwich and took a drink. "Because, I saw them together. I could just tell. Also, I've known Georgia a long time. She's the type to get in a man's pockets."

"Do you think he killed Mrs. Wilde?"

"Hard to say. He certainly has a temper. He basically threw me out of the place when he didn't like my questions."

That sounded like the Marty Fisk she had seen at previous city council meetings. "Are you going to tell the police?"

"Not yet. I don't have enough to go on."

Deena reached in her purse for her billfold. She didn't want Dan to pay for her lunch. "I appreciate your telling me all this. You could have just called me though. You didn't have to go to this much trouble to fill me in."

"Actually, that's not the only reason we're here. I need your help."

"Help with what?"

"With the investigation."

Before Deena could protest, Clara walked up with a Styrofoam box for Deena's leftovers and topped off Dan's coffee.

What on earth did he need her for? He was a seasoned reporter who had won several awards for their small newspaper.

Dan grabbed the check and shoved it in his shirt pocket. "Put your money away."

He said it with such conviction that Deena did as instructed.

"Look, if you help me out with this story, I'm gonna owe you a lot of dinners."

"Haven't you forgotten something?" She sat back and folded her arms. "Pryor banned me from the stories—about Fisk *and* the murder. Not to mention Gary and my lawyer. Why do you need me anyway?"

He pulled his handkerchief out of his pocket and wiped his forehead. "Fisk is doing something wrong, and I want to catch him. It's one thing to build a business. It's another thing to lie and cheat in the process. We don't need people like that running our town."

He made a good point. Outside the window, several semi-trucks flew by on the highway. She turned back to Dan. "You really care about Maycroft, don't you? You could get a job at a major newspaper, but you're still here after all these years chasing down stories."

He put his arm over the back of the booth and smiled. "That's 'cuz I'm too lazy to leave."

Deena shook her head. "You're not lazy. I've seen your work. I used to think you were. Every time I'd drive by Grady's, your Cadillac would be parked out front. But now I know." She shook her head again. "You're not lazy."

He rubbed his hand against his face, seeming uncomfortable with the compliment. "No, I'm not. But, what I am is oldschool. I like to work a story from the back door. When I try to go through the front, half the time they slam it in my face. Sure, I can get answers that way. But I ain't looking for just answers. I'm looking for the true story."

She smiled, knowing just what he meant. This was the kind of reporter she had hoped to be. Rough around the edges and not afraid to get her boots muddy.

He pointed to her. "You're better coming through the front door than I am. They're not smart enough to be afraid of you. Me, on the other hand, they know I'm working an angle. I like to surprise people. Catch 'em off guard. Before they know what I'm doing, I'm done and gone. Got all the story I need." He slapped his hand on the table.

Deena was in awe. This was the longest conversation she'd ever had with the man, yet she felt like she'd known him forever.

Dan took a gulp of coffee and waved his mug at her. "You know, you and I might make a pretty good team if I could stand being around you."

94         LISA B. THOMAS

"Around me?" Her back stiffened." What's wrong with me?"

"Look at yourself. Your hair is all smooth and straight. Looks like you have at least three colors going on in there."

"They're called *highlights*." He was obviously teasing with her. She was more amused than annoyed.

"See, that's another thing. You use big words when you write."

"Such as...?"

"You wrote last week that the town's Easter Egg Hunt would support *philanthropic* endeavors."

Deena waved off Clara's coffee pot. "What's wrong with that?"

"Honey, this town has one foot in the church pew and the other in a pile of manure. You can't swing a dead chicken in this place without hittin' a red-neck." He took another drag from his cup. "There's a lot of people trying to make Maycroft uppity, advertising boutique shops and fine dining. You know as well as I do that most of those waiters at those fancy restaurants chickened out of going into the military and are living in their mommas' attics. Now, they're wearing monkey suits to cover up their painted lady tattoos. They can't pronounce the names of most of the food they're servin' and probably couldn't keep it down if they were forced to eat it."

Deena chuckled at his long-winded diatribe. "You should really write a column—or run for mayor."

He got out of the booth and picked up his jacket. "Nah. Then I wouldn't have anything to crank about."

Coffee sloshed in her stomach as she slid out of the booth. "Let me talk to Gary. I'll call you later." She headed to the door.

Dan stopped at the cash register. "You better not wait too long. We got us some criminals to catch."

IT WAS A LOT HARDER than Deena thought it would be to convince Gary that doing a couple of interviews for Dan would be harmless. She had to play up to his civic-loving nature, citing freedom of the press, *It Takes a Village*, and a couple of George Strait lyrics. Finally, he agreed, saying he hadn't seen her that excited about work since she got a new overhead projector screen in her school classroom. That was back in the '90s.

She down-played the possible connection between Fisk and the murder, knowing it might be too much for her husband to stomach.

Her assignment from Dan was to talk to Georgia and see what she could find out about Fisk and his plan—his real plan, that is. She had already worked out a way to distance herself from Dan and the newspaper. Her strategy was to flatter Georgia into opening up. Women loved to be admired by other women.

But as she pulled into the pawn shop parking lot late that afternoon, Georgia was pulling out in her yellow Mini Cooper. Deena turned her car around and debated what she should do. She still hadn't made it to the antique mall, and glass items were clinking around inside their boxes.

At the last second, Deena decided to follow Georgia. She knew the woman lived in a townhouse on the north side of Maycroft. That's probably where she was going. Out of the corner of her eye, Deena noticed something. Parked at the Palm

Parks motel was a white van just like the one she had noticed the other day. Could it be the same one? She didn't have time to stop and find out.

Georgia stopped at a streetlight, leaving Deena no choice but to pull up behind her. She grabbed her sunglasses and cell phone, lowering her head as though she were deep in conversation.

A few blocks later, Georgia parked and went inside Gail's Nails.

Deena pulled into a space near the side of the building and waited as two minutes clicked off her watch. She got out of the car and went inside. Georgia wasn't at any of the nail stations. On the sign-in book, she had written "pedicure" next to her name. Looked like Deena would be getting her toes done.

As the nail girl led her to the back, Deena motioned toward the empty chair next to Georgia's.

Luckily, Georgia had her nose buried in a magazine and didn't look up until Deena nearly turned over the large tub of hot wax.

Deena sat down and reached for the chair's remote control. Smiling, she looked toward Georgia. "I just love these massage chairs, don't you?"

Without looking up, Georgia gave a quick nod of her head.

Deena thought she sounded like one of those antsy passengers you get stuck next to on an airplane. She turned on the massage action, and a giant ball began rolling up and down her back. When she hit another button, the chair began to vibrate. She set down the remote before she could do any more damage. The roller on her back caused her to sway a little to the front and back. She slid her feet into the hot, soapy water. It was her first pedicure of the season. Her last one had been in late fall when sandal weather blew out of Texas.

She needed to get Georgia's attention. Start up a conversation. "Come here often?" The words came out like gunfire as Deena's teeth chattered from the chair's vibration.

Georgia looked up from her magazine and then over at Deena as if she had two heads.

That was stupid. This wasn't a bar. She reached back and randomly started mashing buttons on the remote. The vibrating stopped, although the rolling seemed to intensify. She tried again. "Don't I know you from somewhere?" Great. Another pick-up line.

Georgia twisted around to look at Deena straight on. "I don't think so." She flipped the pages of her magazine loudly.

Deena tried to calm herself by taking a few cleansing breaths. The girl working on her toenails seemed intent on digging out her cuticles with an ice pick. At least that's how it felt. All the back and forth motion was making her dizzy.

"Didn't I meet you at the pawn shop the other day? I remember that beautiful red hair of yours."

Then Georgia smiled as she looked back at Deena. "Are you that reporter?"

"Yes. I'm Deena Sharpe. I'm not really much of a reporter, though. I just got bumped down to features."

Georgia took the bait. "Too bad. Dan Carson came by yesterday. He's a first-class jerk. I can't believe I ever dated him."

"Tell me about it. I mean…about him being a jerk. You'd have to be crazy to go out with him." Oops. Wrong thing to say.

Georgia turned back to her magazine.

Deena lowered her eyes. The foot warrior had pulled out the extra-large cheese grater and was determined to extract a pound of flesh from Deena's feet. *What does she do, work out before coming here? Lighten up, lady.* She clenched her teeth, wondering if that was a drop of blood she saw floating in the water.

Finally, it was time for the lotion massage. Deena snickered at the girl. *Too bad for you I haven't shaved my legs since a Bush was president. Serves you right.*

As if the magazine were trash, Georgia tossed it on the floor and leaned back with her eyes closed.

Deena thought a minute, and then tried again. "I can't believe you dated Dan. He's looks to be twice your age."

Georgia opened her eyes and cocked her head. "We all make mistakes."

Deena started to ask if she were seeing anyone now, but realized she might end up engaged to the woman if she weren't careful. She took a different approach. "I was really looking forward to talking to your boss, Councilman Fisk, about his rezoning plan. I think it sounds like a terrific idea."

"Really? It'll make a fortune, you know."

She was back on the hook. Now all Deena had to do was reel her in and throw her in the boat. Just then, a wave of nausea came over her. Between the boat rocking motion and the girl banging her fists up and down Deena's calves, she felt seasick. It was all she could do not to lose her lunch right there in the footbath. She must have turned green because the nail girl reached up and turned off the massage chair.

"What color?" the girl asked.

Deena realized she had forgotten to choose a polish before she sat down. That was a big no-no when it came to pedi-etiquette. "Just use whatever you have in your drawer." She turned back to Georgia who was admiring the lime green polish being applied to her toes.

"Bold color choice," Deena said.

Georgia tossed her red hair off her shoulder. "I'm a bold woman."

"What do you think they will build on that property if the city re-zones? I'd love to see an outlet mall there."

"Build? Nothing is being built. He's—" Georgia clamped her mouth shut, and her neck turned the color of her hair.

Her toenails were finished and the girl sprayed them with a fast-drying aerosol.

Georgia quickly slipped on her sandals, seeming to use the interruption as an excuse to end their conversation. "Sorry. I have to get back to work."

It was Deena's turn to stare with her mouth gaped open. What had Georgia meant? What was she hiding? Wasn't Fisk planning to build on the property? The woman had been close to spilling the beans. Deena needed to get out of there and call Dan.

Looking down at her feet, she did a double-take. Staring back were ten little piggies dressed in fluorescent purple party clothes. Deena glared at the girl. To add insult to injury, she'd have to leave the shop wearing yellow foam thongs since she'd left the house wearing loafers. She couldn't go to her booth wearing those.

As she waddled to the front door, she grimaced at her predicament. How on earth did Miss Marple manage to solve all those crimes without humiliating herself?

# Chapter 14

**A**s usual, Roscoe was right. The buzzer rang non-stop on Saturday as women lined up and down the street in front of the house waiting to have their fortunes told by Sister Natasha.

After just a few hours, she had a booming headache. Roscoe had bought scented candles by mistake, and the smell was overpowering. Still, it was worth it. At forty bucks a pop per customer, they were making a fortune.

At around two o'clock, Tonya ate a ham sandwich and washed it down with a beer. To get the alcohol smell out of her mouth, she went in the bathroom to brush her teeth. Her make-up still looked good.

"Are you ready?" Roscoe asked just as she was spitting out the toothpaste.

"Sure." She wiped her mouth and applied a quick swath of lipstick. As she walked into the kitchen to stand in her place behind the curtain, she heard Roscoe talking to the latest customer.

His usual short responses seemed longer.

Wondering if something was wrong, Tonya peeked through the slit in the curtain to see who was on the other side. Far from the frumpy women who usually came to see her, this girl wore tight jeans with rhinestones on the pockets and a pearl-snap shirt. She had dark, wavy hair that fell past her shoulders.

Was Roscoe actually smiling at her? Tonya rankled when she saw him offer his arm and escort her to the table. What a jerk! Her first thought was to bust through the curtain and smack him in the head. When he called her name and headed her way, she stopped.

"Who is that?" Tonya whispered as he came around the corner.

"Why are you standing here? That was your cue!"

"Were you flirting with her?" Tonya's eyes sparked as she glared at him.

"Don't be ridiculous," he replied, pushing her into the room.

Instead of her usual sweep, she walked slowly, eyeing the young girl who seemed lost in her own thoughts. When Tonya sat down, she noticed tears winding their way down the girl's cheeks.

She spoke her scripted line. "You come see Sister Natasha. Why?"

The girl sniffed and dabbed her clear blue eyes with a tissue.

Tonya couldn't believe those were her real lashes. Nothing moved and nothing smeared.

"I'm here about my grandmother. She was...murdered a few days ago." The word stuck in her throat. "I want to know if you can tell me who killed her."

Tonya hesitated. This was not the kind of question she was expecting. Murder? In this po-dunk town?

"What name?" Tonya heard a soft gasp from the other side of the curtain. She knew Roscoe would be mad, but she didn't care.

The girl wrung her hands in her lap. "My name or my grandmother's?"

"Both."

"My name is Katy Wilde. My grandmother is—was—Barbara Wilde."

Tonya used her thickest accent. "You have boyfriend?"

Katy's eyes widened. "Yes. Why? Are you saying he killed my grandmother?" Her hands began to shake and her words came out in short gasps.

"No. Maybe." Tonya realized she had the perfect chance to scare Roscoe away from this girl. "He mad at grandmother?"

Katy caught her breath. "How did you know? He wasn't mad, but he was upset." She leaned in closer as though sharing a secret with her best girlfriend. "He's married, you see. And my family is Catholic. My grandmother was super Catholic, if you know what I mean. She would never approve of me marrying a divorced man. That's why we had to keep our relationship a secret. That, and he didn't want to tell his wife until I was free to be with him."

There were so many things Tonya wanted to ask her, but she couldn't. Like, why would someone as gorgeous as you waste your time with a married man? Or, why hasn't he just left his wife if he really loves you? And, especially, are you sure he didn't kill off granny so he could marry you?

Tonya considered her options. She had no idea who killed Katy's grandmother, but she might as well put the girl on the right track just in case it was the no-good cheater. She placed the deck of playing cards in the middle of the table. "Mix."

Tonya could feel Katy watching her intently as she went through her mumbling routine. When she revealed Katy's two cards, she caught her breath and shook her head. "Natasha see man. No face. Natasha see..." She realized she forgot to ask Katy how her grandmother died. She'd have to wing it. "Natasha see evil man. Run! Run away from evil man!" She blew out the candles and covered her face with her hands.

The tears began to flow. "What else? Do you see anything else? Who is this man?" Katy grasped the sides of the table and rocked its wobbly legs.

"Natasha sees no more. Go. Go!"

Katy got up and headed to the front door. She stopped and turned back to Tonya. "Thank you, Sister Natasha. Bless you."

Like a shot in the dark, Roscoe was around the curtain and into the room, eyes blazing. "What was that about?"

Tonya stuck out her chin defiantly. "I heard you talking to her. I saw the way you looked at her."

"You're crazy. I was just doing my job." The buzzer rang at the door.

Tonya stood up and brushed past him back to the kitchen. "So was I."

When she was safely behind the security of the curtain, her knees grew weak. She couldn't risk losing Roscoe and being left alone again. She would do whatever it took to hold on to him.

# Chapter 15

Western bars were not really their scene. Deena and Gary preferred having a nice glass of wine at a quiet restaurant on a Saturday night. But Deena used her power of persuasion to convince Gary that going to the Hitchin' Post Saloon was part of her research for the story she was working on with Dan.

He reluctantly agreed to go, saying he could at least keep his eye on her that way. Otherwise, she'd end up going with Sandra, and he knew how the two of them could manage to get in trouble when left to their own devices.

Dan had been intrigued by the bit of information Deena had managed to wrangle out of Georgia. It confirmed that Fisk's plan was self-serving and not for the good of the town. Now they needed to talk to Katy. Knowing Mrs. Wilde's granddaughter would need the kid glove treatment, he left it to Deena to arrange a time to meet with her.

After talking it over with Gary, Deena thought it would be better to catch Katy at work rather than just showing up at her house. Katy couldn't slam the door in her face in a public place.

Saturday evening, Deena felt like she was back in college when she and her friends would go out dancing. Piles of shoes in the back of her closet had somehow multiplied. She spied the tops of her dusty cowboy boots and pulled them out. They were turquoise and brown with pointy toes and had the smell of rich leather.

Normally, she would wear a western skirt, white blouse, and fringed shawl. She had a favorite concho belt that looked great with her silver jewelry. She had last worn that outfit to Billy Bob's in Ft. Worth to celebrate Gary's birthday. However, it was much too fancy for the Hitchin' Post. Besides, she knew whatever she wore would reek of cigarette smoke by the time she got home. She opted for a pair of jeans and a tunic instead. She had an old suede jacket that might still fit.

Gary called from the garage where he kicked dried mud off his boots. "You ready?"

"Yes. What do you think?" She performed a clumsy ballet twirl.

He cocked his head. "Are you sure that jacket still fits?"

The smile fell from her face. "Thanks for the compliment. I didn't want to wear my red raincoat."

"I'm sorry. You look great. Now let's get going." He smacked her bottom as she walked past.

They were early enough to find a dirty, but open, table. Gary carried off the empty beer bottles as Deena grabbed a wad of napkins to wipe off spilled beer and peanut shells. She thought about the days when they were more likely to just put the dirty stuff on the floor and wipe the table with a sleeve. Their age was showing.

Gary sat down and looked for a waitress. "Should we wait, or should I go up to the bar?"

Deena leaned over to hear him above the sound of Willie Nelson blaring through the speakers. "Let's wait. I can ask the waitress to point out Katy Wilde."

After a few minutes of checking out the crowd, a girl in cut-off shorts and boots walked up to their table. "What can I get you?" She tugged at the red-checkered blouse tied around her mid-section.

"A couple of Coors Lights," Gary said.

"We only have Budweiser. Bud Light okay?"

He nodded and she pranced off to the bar. Gary rolled his eyes. "Nice place. We should come here more often."

Deena gave him a shot to the arm. "Relax. We might as well have fun."

"Fun would be sitting at home watching a basketball game or going to the movies."

She agreed. If it weren't for her interest in talking to Katy, she'd probably be curled up in her pajamas and watching a movie in the bed with Hurley.

The waitress returned with their drinks. She leaned down a little lower than necessary toward Gary. "Do you want to pay for these now or start a tab?"

Without checking with Deena, he reached in his pocket and pulled out some cash.

Deena motioned to the waitress. "Can you tell me where to find Katy Wilde?"

"Sure, she's behind the bar. There." She pointed to a pretty brunette.

Deena studied the young woman for a moment. Several groups of people walked in and obstructed her view. She leaned toward Gary. "It's just going to get busier. Maybe I should go talk to her now."

"Good idea."

Deena picked up her bottle and weaved her way through the tables. There was an open stool at the bar, so she grabbed it.

As she sat down, the man next to her turned and gave her an exaggerated eyeing, checking her out from head to toe. "Well, aren't you the handsomest woman in these parts." His voice boomed, and several other patrons turned to look. His rancid beer breath nearly knocked her off the stool.

Annoyed at the attention, Deena shot him her best brush-off face and fixed her eyes on Katy, hoping telepathy would make the girl look her way.

Katy worked quickly and quietly, filling orders as the waitresses called them out over the din.

"Buy you a beer?" Slim Pickens obviously didn't get the message.

Deena held up her left hand and jiggled her wedding ring with her thumb.

He flopped his arm across her shoulder. "Oh, you're married! That doesn't stop us from getting together around here! Does it, Katy?"

The girl's eyes shot daggers, and she nodded to someone standing off to the side of the room. As quick as lightning, a burly man grabbed Slim by the shoulders and escorted him to the door. Deena heard a bit of discussion about calling for a ride. Then they were gone.

"Sorry about that," Katy said as she wiped the bar in front of Deena.

"Thanks. Not your fault." Deena didn't want to waste any time. "Are you Katy?"

"Yes." She crinkled her face. "Do I know you?"

"No. I'm Deena Sharpe." She reached her hand across the counter, and Katy gave it a shake.

"Your name is familiar, but I can't think of where I've heard it."

Deena leaned forward and lowered her voice. "I work for the Tribune. I'm the one who found your grandmother."

Katy covered her mouth and stood motionless.

Deena knew she had to talk fast before she got the boot and ended up on the pavement with Slim. "I'm so sorry for your loss. Really." She shook her head sympathetically. "I was hoping to talk to you in private. I'm anxious to find out who killed your grandmother."

Deena was prepared for three reactions. One, Katy might blow up at her for sticking her nose in. A possible sign of guilt. Two, she might be angry, blaming Deena. A stage of grief. Or three, she might agree to meet with her, desperate to find some answers.

Luckily, it was the third. Katy regained her composure and nodded toward the end of the bar.

Deena stood up and glanced over at Gary who was watching her every move. She walked over to Katy.

"I'm off tomorrow. I'll be at my grandmother's house all afternoon. Come by then."

Deena smiled, nodding in agreement. She headed out the door with Gary on her heels.

"Leaving so soon?" Gary mocked as they walked toward the car.

"I did it. I got her to agree to talk to me. I'm meeting her tomorrow afternoon."

"Great." He opened her door and bowed as though welcoming a princess into his carriage. "The night's still young, though. Want to go to a movie?"

"Sure. As long as it's not a comedy. I'm in the mood for a good mystery."

# Chapter 16

As soon as she walked in the door after church, Deena pulled off her slacks and heels and headed for the bedroom. "I thought Rev. Marino would never quit today. I can't even imagine what he's planning for Easter."

Gary picked up the TV remote, a move that was almost mechanical when his feet hit the hardwood floor of the den. "I think in the spring he feels like he has to make up for cutting services short in the fall so everyone can get home in time to watch the Cowboys."

"Maybe so. Would you mind making us a couple of sandwiches? I want to hurry up and get over to see Katy. And remember, you're not the sandwich-Picasso. Just slap everything on there and be done with it."

It must be true that opposites attract. Gary was neat and deliberate in everything he did. His extreme attention to detail made him an accountant extraordinaire, but Deena often found it tedious to wait for him to complete a simple task like brushing his teeth or sorting the laundry.

Since the dark skies had finally cleared, it was warm enough for crop pants. Pulling them out for the first time was a spring ritual, much like planting petunias or changing the batteries in the smoke alarms.

Inside what would have been a walk-in closet if it hadn't been piled high with boxes of who-knows-whats, colorful blouses tempted her, but none matched the purple toenails sprouting from her sandals. She wondered what the inside of Georgia Parks closet must look like. Obviously, Deena wasn't as bold a dresser. She finally decided on a white top and her khaki pants. She looked in the full-length mirror. All she was missing was a My Little Pony doll.

She scarfed down her sandwich, offering her compliments to the chef. After a quick peck on Gary's cheek, she was off to do some real investigative work.

Barbara Wilde's street seemed even more depressing than when she had been there a few days earlier. Lawns that should have been covered in new growth were brown and muddy. Dead branches were cracked and hung from the trees with no new buds popping out. Clouds appeared out of nowhere and cast shadows over the houses.

Deena parked and went up the steps to the front door. She shivered as a deja-vu moment came over her. The door was open this time, though, so she peered through the screen to see Katy sitting on the floor cross-legged surrounded by photo albums. Deena called her name, and the girl jumped.

"Oh, it's you." She got up and walked over to unlatch the screen door. "Come on in."

The rocking chair where Deena had found Mrs. Wilde was noticeably gone.

Katy seemed to read her thoughts. "I had the police get rid of it."

Deena nodded and took a seat on the floral sofa as Katy plopped back down on the floor.

Deena felt a sneeze coming on. "Ah-ah-choo!"

"Bless you."

"Does a cat live here?" she asked, digging in her purse for a tissue.

"No, but sometimes Mrs. Canfield's cat comes in through the open window."

"I see." She wiped her nose. "What are you working on?"

"I'm supposed to be boxing up Gran's stuff to be thrown out or given to charity. I just can't seem to make myself do it." She ran her hand lightly across the books surrounding her. "So many memories."

A lump knotted in Deena's throat. She remembered when she lost her own grandparents. "It's only been a few days. Maybe you should wait a while to tackle it."

"I wish I could. It's just that my brother is pressuring me to sell the place. He'd have it sold tomorrow if I let him."

Deena remembered what Dan had said about the police not being able to find Katy's brother. "Does he live in town?"

"No, he lives outside of Houston. The only thing he seems to care about is the money. He's always got money problems." She pulled up a cardboard box and began stacking the albums inside.

Deena saw her opening to bring up Fisk. "I don't want to sound rude or anything, but this house—in this neighbor-hood—I doubt you could make much money selling it."

Katy shook her head. "That's what I thought. But Gran told me someone had offered her a lot for it not that long ago."

"Did she say who the buyer was or what would happen to the house?"

"It was through a realtor. Apparently, it was a businessman who had already bought some of the other houses in the area."

Deena's pulse quickened. "Why didn't she take the offer?"

"My grandmother was born in this house. She got married here. She wanted me to raise my children here. She'd never sell it." Katy walked up to an oak hutch and opened the doors. A mishmash of old dishes stared back at her. She put her hands on her hips and sighed.

Old dishes were right up Deena's alley. She would keep her eye out for anything collectible and let Katy know its value. She picked up a couple of boxes and walked over to help. "Do you have any newspaper?"

Katy pointed to the kitchen table.

Deena took the lead and started wrapping plates in paper and putting them in the boxes.

Picking up a chipped cup, Katy studied it for a moment and then wrapped it up.

They worked without talking for several minutes before Deena broke the silence. "Have you come up with any ideas about who may have killed her?"

The question hung in the air for a long moment. "Just one. And I can't believe I'm even thinking about it."

"Who is it?"

"My...boyfriend." Just as she said it, a teacup fell from her hands and smashed at their feet. "Oh dear!"

"Don't move," Deena said, looking down at Katy's bare feet. "Where's a broom?"

"In the kitchen."

Deena found a closet and got the broom and dustpan. She swept up an area next to Katy so she could step away and get her shoes. A small shard of glass had stuck in her ankle and was bleeding. "You go take care of your foot, and I'll take care of this," Deena said.

As she swept, a creaking noise drew Deena's attention back toward the kitchen. She walked in to see a man coming down the narrow wooden staircase. Maybe this was the boyfriend.

"Who are you?" he asked, stopping before getting to the bottom step. Luckily, he was wearing tennis shoes along with his jeans.

"Be careful, there's glass." She emptied the dustpan in the trashcan. "I'm Deena. And you are..."

"Where's my sister?"

So, this was the brother.

"I'm here," Katy said, coming from around the corner. "Deena Sharpe, this is my rude brother, Travis."

"Whatever," he said, leaning against the handrail. "What's going on down here?"

"She's helping me pack." Katy folded her arms as if daring him to say something back.

"I have to finish getting dressed. Hope there's something to eat here." He turned and clomped back up the stairs.

"Sorry. I can't seem to get away from inconsiderate men. Except for Ned." As soon as she said the name, she caught her breath and the color drained from her face.

Deena picked up on the situation immediately. "Is Ned married?"

Katy shook her head.

Deena motioned toward the table. "Let's sit down and have a glass of iced tea."

Katy followed her. "There's a pitcher in the refrigerator."

"As there should be in every southern home." She pulled out the pitcher. "Is it sweet or unsweet?"

"It's sweet."

"Just the way I like it." Turning her back, Deena opened a cabinet looking for glasses. She used that moment to pull out her cell phone and send a quick text message to Dan. "Brother here."

She filled the glasses with ice and carried them to the table. "So where do you want to start? With the possible killer or with the boyfriend?"

Katy took a gulp of tea and looked sheepishly over the top of her glass.

Deena set her glass down and crossed her legs. "Tell me."

"I don't know why I'm telling you anything. I just met you. But I have no one else to talk to, and you said you wanted to help."

"I do. I'll be honest. I'm a journalist, and I'm working on this as a story. But I found your grandmother dead—in this house—in my own town. I want to find the killer as much as you do."

"But my secrets..."

"*Everyone* has secrets. I'm not going to reveal anything that isn't important to the case. I'm not a cop."

Tears dripped from Katy's eyes as she stared into Deena's. She must have found trust there because she began to open up. "I went to that psychic. Sister Natasha. I told her how my grandmother was Catholic and wouldn't approve of me marrying a divorced man. She looked at the cards and said that he may have killed Gran to be able to marry me."

Deena was confused. "So is he married or divorced?"

"He's still married. He's waiting to get divorced until I agree to marry him."

Deena tilted her head sympathetically and started to speak, but Katy interrupted.

"I know how that sounds. Like he was just playing me. But it's not like that. He loves me."

Wanting to lecture her on the evils of dating married men, Deena decided to bite her tongue. "And Sister Natasha said he murdered your grandmother?"

"Well, not exactly. She said it was a man and implied that it could be him."

Deena remembered what Kristy had said at the salon. "I thought all she did was tell customers their fortunes. Told them what would happen in the future."

Katy shrugged her shoulders. "Not with me."

Even after witnessing Natasha find the Coleman boy, Deena still had some doubts about her psychic powers. In this case though, she might be right. "It sounds like Ned—I mean your boyfriend, could have a motive. Do you think it's possible he did it?"

"That's the thing. He's not like that. He's sweet and gentle. I couldn't imagine him just showing up and strangling her with her own scarf." She rubbed her face. "He's an accountant. He plans everything right down to the last dot and diddle."

Deena stifled a laugh. She knew exactly what the girl meant. "Still, you need to tell the police your suspicions."

Katy's brown eyes doubled in size. "I can't! At least not yet."

"Besides not wanting the affair to be public, what are you waiting for?"

"For him to pop the question. Maybe he's just being sensitive, but when I mentioned that my grandmother's passing meant we could get married, he didn't want to talk about it. He hasn't called me since then."

The writing was like neon graffiti on the old brick wall as far as Deena was concerned. Ned had used the grandmother as an excuse to string the poor child along. Now, he was going to have to invent another delay tactic. Maybe the dog ate his homework. Regardless, Deena didn't have the heart to suggest it to Katy, at least not without more proof.

"You don't really believe in this psychic stuff, do you?" Deena hoped the question wasn't too harsh.

Katy looked mournfully around the room with its cracked ceilings and peeling paint. "I don't know what to believe anymore or who to believe in. You know, Gran said she thought this house was haunted. In the last few months she started hearing and finding strange things. A few weeks ago—"

"Ding-dong! Are you there? Anybody home?" A woman's voice coming through the front screen door sang out through the house.

Katy craned to see around the corner. "Who could that be? I'll be back."

As she opened the front door, Travis barreled down the steps and blew past Deena toward the front door. Deena stood in the doorway of the dining room with a clear view of the den. She immediately recognized the caller.

Katy stood in front of the screen door when Travis reached around and opened it. "You must be the realtor, Charla Hicks," he said and waved her inside.

"I am indeedy," she chortled as she waltzed into the room carrying a brown leather satchel.

Deena couldn't believe all that bleached hair fit through the doorway. She suddenly felt like Boo Radley standing unnoticed in the corner of the Finch's house. It was the closest she'd ever come to being a fly on the wall. The feeling was more dizzying than a second margarita.

Katy's face revealed a mixture of confusion and annoyance. "What's this all about?"

Travis beamed and flashed a pearly smile. "She's a realtor. We have an offer on the house!"

Katy scoffed. "An offer? I didn't even know it was for sale yet?"

Making herself at home, Charla took off her jacket and threw her satchel on the sofa. She'd obviously been there before. "Who'd have imagined this was such a hot property? But I have a buyer and he's ready to play. Let's sit." She sat down and was joined by Travis, whose bounce would rival an excited Tigger's.

Katy sat in an upholstered wingback across from them. Her sour expression took some of the glow from the room.

Charla pulled a manila folder from her bag. "Now to be clear, this offer is slightly less than the buyer offered your grandmother a few months back."

Travis bristled. "Less? Why?"

"Because, my dear, a woman was murdered here. That has to be disclosed. No one wants to buy a haunted house."

"So the buyer is planning to live in the house?" Katy asked.

"I don't know that for sure. It shouldn't really matter though. Once you sell, they can do whatever they want, as long as the sheriff doesn't catch 'em!" She gave Travis a flirty wink.

"You're right. It doesn't matter," Travis said. "What's the offer? And skip all that realtor garbage. Bottom line."

"I just *looove* to see an anxious seller!" She turned to the last page of the packet. "Bottom line. One hundred thousand dollars."

"Sold!" Travis yelled and jumped up from the sofa.

"Wait a minute! I haven't agreed to anything yet. I'm Gran's executor. She's barely been in the ground a day, and you're already trying to cash in on her death."

Travis kicked at the box of photo albums. "What are you talking about? That's a lot of money for this broken down pile of lumber. Half of that is yours."

"Have you forgotten that she made us promise not to sell the house?"

"You promised, maybe. I didn't. What do you care anyway? Are you planning to live here?"

Katy stood up. "Maybe I am."

Travis moved to within inches of his sister and held out his hand. "Fine. Hand over fifty thousand dollars and you can rot here for all I care."

Katy's mouth flopped open.

Charla stood up and gathered her papers. "Well, it looks like you two have some things to talk over. I'll just leave my card here on the table and wait to hear from you." She opened the front door and looked back at the two of them staring each other down like kids in a playground scuffle. "The offer expires in three days, so don't take too long to decide. Ta-ta."

The screen door slammed behind her, causing Deena to jump. She started to move out of the shadows when Travis walked toward the front door. "I'm outta here. I'll be back when you've cooled down."

"Stop! There's one more thing." Katy pulled her cell phone from her pocket. "I got a call yesterday from a life insurance company. Seems you took a policy out on Gran. Care to explain?"

Travis' brow furrowed as he snarled. If it were possible for steam to come out of his ears, he could have fueled a locomotive. "I *didn't* take a policy out on her. I just picked up the payments. She was going to let it lapse. I've spent a hundred bucks a month for the past two years paying on that thing."

"I see. And who are the beneficiaries?"

"Beneficiary, single. Me." He opened the screen door and bolted from the house.

Deena rushed over to Katy and caught her by the arm, worried she was about to collapse onto the well-worn rug. Before she got her to the chair, a siren blared outside the house and lit up the room with flashes of red and blue. They both hurried back to the door.

A police car and Detective Evans' sedan pulled up and blocked the driveway where Travis had started to back out. Trapped like a rat, he rolled down his window.

Evans walked up to the window flashing his badge. "Travis Wilde. Detective Evans, Maycroft PD. We'd like to ask you a few questions." And in the blink of an eye, Travis was getting into the back of the squad car.

"Do you think he's under arrest?" Katy asked.

"No. They'd have had him in handcuffs."

Katy glanced at her cell phone and walked back toward the kitchen.

Deena looked next door in time to see Millie Canfield hoist a baseball bat onto her shoulder and close her front door with a decided bang. Wooden bats must be the weapon of choice in this area. Deena had noticed one leaning in the corner by the back door in Katy's kitchen.

Just as she was about to go back inside, tires squealed and a vehicle sped down the street in the direction of the police cars. It was the white paneled van.

"YOU CALLED THEM, DIDN'T you?" Deena asked as she pulled into her garage. She wasn't sure if she should be mad at Dan or not.

"Yes. Had to."

She switched her phone from one ear to the next, hoping she'd hear a different answer. "Why?"

"That's how it works in this business. You give them a tip. They give you one. It'll pay off, trust me."

"Katy thought I called the police. I convinced her it was probably her nosy neighbor. I think she bought it." She stared at a dent in front of her on the garage wall that she had forgotten about. Gary always warned her about pulling the car in too far.

"What else did she say? Any suspects?"

Deena told him about the psychic reader, the married boyfriend, the offer on the house, and the insurance policy. "My gut says the offer was from Fisk. The realtor said the same buyer had made another offer not that long ago."

She gave him the Cliff Notes version of the information, knowing Gary would be out to check on her any minute. Hurley—the snitch— was barking on the other side of the door to the house. "So where do we go from here?"

"I think the boyfriend is a longshot, but we should try to check him out. Can you get his full name?"

"I don't have to. I'm pretty sure I know who he is."

When Gary opened the door, Deena held up a finger to signal she'd be just a minute.

"Okay. See what you can find out. I'm going to see what they have on the brother. Sounds circumstantial, especially if he has an alibi for Tuesday night. Let's get together tomorrow and compare notes. We may need to pay a visit to the neighbor."

Deena opened her car door to get out. "Call me."

"You done good today, cutie."

When she hung up, she was a tossed salad of emotions. The adrenaline rush had subsided, and she was left with the leafy greens. Katy was counting on her to help find the killer. She wanted to help, but she felt way out of her comfort zone. Maybe she should have listened to Pryor and stuck to her own stories.

*Pryor!* He was expecting a story on Sister Natasha, and she hadn't even stepped foot in the door. So much for lazy days at boring yawn-fests. First order of business tomorrow would be to pay a visit to the quack shack and see what skeletons she could uncover. She was determined to go at this story with an open mind. Unfortunately, when it came to psychics, she didn't have one.

# Chapter 17

Occasionally in Texas, a weird phenomenon would occur when the sky could look practically clear but rain would still find its way to the ground. Of course, there might have been a cloud over there a ways, but surely that wasn't where the water originated. Such a day greeted Deena as she pulled up in front of Sister Natasha's little house on Monday morning.

She had waited until ten o'clock, having no idea when the paranormally-gifted rolled out of bed. By the line of cars already in front of the house, it looked like the clairvoyance racket was akin to dairy farming. She pulled up as close as she could get.

A hand-written sign on the front door was too small to see from her vantage point of umpteen cars back, so she got out to read it. The question was...to umbrella or not to umbrella? She stared straight up, wondering where in the heck those raindrops were coming from. If she could serpentine in just the right fashion, she would avoid getting wet altogether. She opted for the skull and crossbones and a direct route.

Moisture had caused some of the ink to drip in ghoulish blood fashion, but the message was still legible. She was to take a number from the pile rubber-banded in a shoebox next to the door. That explained everyone sitting in their cars. She counted the other vehicles, trying to calculate if it was going to be worth her time to wait. The front door opened and out popped a smiling woman clutching her handbag, dancing toward the street. Deena hadn't seen such blatant public enthusiasm since the Chamber of Commerce announced it was increasing the city-wide Easter Egg Hunt by a hundred eggs.

"You're supposed to take a number," a dark figure growled from inside the house.

"I know. I was trying to figure out how long I would have to wait," Deena said. She felt like she had gotten caught trying to cut in line in the school cafeteria.

"Time waits for no man."

Deena smiled at the shadow. "Chaucer, right?"

"No, Roscoe." He shut the door and the smell of jasmine wafted up her nose.

*Who's Roscoe?* After a glimpse at the gate-keeper, she was determined to view the inner sanctum. She picked up a number and headed back to wait in her car.

The front door opened again, and she turned around to see an arm appear holding a paper with the number twelve on it. She had number nineteen. As she got back in the car, she saw a familiar figure dashing toward the porch. It was Betty, the librarian. *Hmm. It's always the quiet types.*

The older she got, the more that naps seemed like little gifts from God. She leaned back the car seat and closed her eyes. She might as well make the most of her wait.

What seemed like only a minute had actually been an hour. She jumped as a rapping sound brought her back from the dead.

"Hey lady. Are you number nineteen? Hurry up or you're going to lose your turn."

Her head was foggier than a London sky. She reached for her purse and the paper card. The sporadic raindrops had morphed into a drizzle. She didn't bother with her umbrella this time. She sprinted to the door and pushed the buzzer. The door opened slowly. Was that a man-made creak she heard or was it original to the house?

Her plan was to present herself as an ordinary customer—if there were such a thing—and then after her reading, announce that she was a reporter wanting to schedule an interview. That way, she would get the full-blown, hokey-pokey, smoke-and-mirrors experience.

The same character who had spoken to her before motioned for her to enter. The room was dark except for candles on a small table. She blinked, trying to adjust her eyes to the dark.

A white palm appeared in front of her. "Forty dollars."

"Do you take credit cards? Just kidding." She pulled out her wallet, barely able to see the dollar amounts on the bills she retrieved. "Nice place you have here."

No response from the butler.

She handed him the cash and followed as he walked in slow motion toward the far side of the table.

He pulled out the chair for her.

She sat down and put her purse on the floor. "I'll have a gin and tonic."

Still nothing. Obviously, they took this paranormal stuff seriously. She would have to control her nervous talking.

The butler walked over to the corner of the room and croaked out, "*Sis-ter Na-ta-sha.*"

By this time, Deena's eyes had adjusted enough to see that there were blankets hung over the front windows, keeping the room bat cave dark. After he disappeared through the curtain, Natasha came out and sat across from her. They locked eyes, and it was clear to Deena that the girl recognized her.

"You come back to Sister Natasha. Why? More missing boy?"

The heat from the candle was starting to burn Deena's face. She pushed it farther off to the side.

"You remember me. I'm here for a reading...or a card trick... or whatever."

"You not believe Natasha's powers."

"Is that a question or a statement?" She bit her lip, not wanting to be tossed out by the butler/bouncer. "Of course I believe. I saw how you found that little boy. I've just never done this before, so I'm a little nervous."

Natasha looked doubtful, but then placed the playing cards on the table. "Mix."

Deena shuffled and bridged the cards three times before setting them back down.

"You have question for Natasha?" She picked up the deck and held it with both hands.

"Should I carry my umbrella tomorrow?" Oops. "Just kidding. Seriously, I have an important question. Can you tell me who killed Barbara Wilde?"

Natasha stared. She set down the cards. "Natasha no find killers."

"But there was a girl here last week. She asked you about her grandmother. You told her the killer was a man."

"Natasha no find killers! You have other question or no?" Her knuckles whitened as she clenched her hands around the cards.

"How about this? Do you know what my job is?" Deena cocked her head.

"Natasha not mind-reader! Natasha see future. Tell fortune."

"I work for the *Northeast Texas Tribune*. I'm a reporter."

"Not for long. Go. Go!" She pointed toward the door.

"I just want to set up an interview. People are interested in new businesses in town. Can I come back?"

Natasha stood up. Despite the darkness in the room, Deena could tell by the movement of her body and the quiver in her voice that she was shaking. "Go now!"

The butler rushed into the room and caught Deena by the arm, practically dragging her out the door. He slapped two twenty dollar bills in her hand and pushed her out the door. Just before it closed behind her, he stuck his head out and whispered, "Leave your card in the box. I'll call you."

Deena stood dumb-founded. Either he was a smart businessman looking for free publicity, or he knew something about the murder. Either way, she was excited.

Ducking her head, she ran back to her car through the rain. She had finally gotten a good look at his face and had a feeling his mustache wasn't the only thing about him that was crooked.

THE HIGHWAY CAFÉ WAS not exactly a parking garage, but Deena still felt like Bob Woodward going to meet Deep Throat when she pulled into the gravel lot. Dan was in "their booth" by the front window. He was already eating.

When she came through the door, she hung her raincoat and umbrella on the coat rack.

Clara headed over to the table armed with hot coffee. "What can I get you?"

Deena gave her a Dan-style salute. "The usual."

"Huh?"

"I mean, a club sandwich. And I'll have iced tea instead of coffee."

Clara glanced at Dan who shot back a half-grin.

"So, you're digging this investigative stuff, I see." He picked diced onions off his burger.

"This is just like I thought it would be." She pulled out several napkins and pushed her tableware off to the side.

"You realized there aren't that many serious crimes in Maycroft, don't you?"

"I guess. Not that I'm sad about it or anything. You know what I mean."

He chuckled and took a bite of his burger. Grease dribbled down his chin and onto the plate.

Deena handed him a wad of napkins. She had filled him in about her visit to Natasha over the phone, but he still had a few questions.

"This guy at the door—the butler—"

"That's just what I called him. I've heard he might be Natasha's brother."

"He was wearing a disguise?"

"Seemed to be. His mustache was obviously fake, and he had on make-up. Weird hair."

Dan waved a French fry. "So he's either playing a part or trying not to be recognized."

"Or both."

Clara brought Deena's sandwich and glass of tea. "More coffee?" she asked Dan.

"You bet, sugar."

They waited for her to return with the coffee then walk back to the counter.

"I wonder what his story is," Dan said. "By the way, did you know they're working out of one of Marty Fisk's rentals?"

"Really? You know, now that you mention it, I think Marty said something about that at the council meeting. Interesting."

Dan wiped his hands and reached out to put his plate on an empty table. He pulled a small notepad from his shirt pocket and flipped through the pages. "Let's decide exactly what to ask the neighbor, Mrs. Canfield. I made some notes."

"Do you know if she saw anything the night of the murder? Did she tell the police anything?" Deena pulled the toothpick off her sandwich and took a bite.

"Nothing. Which was unusual in itself. The killer must have gone in stealth because she swears she didn't hear anything." He looked at his notes. "I'm going to ask about Fisk and any offers to buy her property. Also, if she has any idea why a buyer might want it."

"Can you add something to your notes for me?"

"Sure. What?" He held his pencil at the ready.

"Ask her if she's ever noticed a suspicious white paneled van. My gut tells me there's something suspicious about it, and she just might have the answer."

MILLIE CANFIELD HAD lived in her house longer than Deena had been alive. She and Barbara were on-again, off-again best friends, depending on whose dog was digging under whose fence and which tree roots were growing into whose pipes. Lately, they'd been "off."

Deena thought for sure Mrs. Canfield was going to slam the door in their faces.

She made them both show her their Tribune ID, driver's license, and a major credit card. Deena was anticipating having to reveal her social security number and birthmarks when the old woman reluctantly allowed them entrance into her home.

"Sit down. Excuse this old housedress. I didn't know I'd be having company." She turned off the television. "Just move Chester out the way. He's an old cat and can't hear anymore. Can I get you some iced tea?"

"No thanks," Deena said, tickled by the question. Typical Southern woman. Offers ice tea no matter the circumstances. "We appreciate your taking time to talk to us. We just want to ask some questions about Barbara Wilde."

Millie sat down in a padded rocker, her hands clenched in her lap. "I can't believe she's gone. She's been my dearest friend for...ever. I thought we would end up in the same retirement home together. We even talked about it. Once when my boy was here, he drove us out to Sunset Gardens, and–"

Dan interrupted. "You say you talked about moving? I thought Barbara was determined never to sell her house. Was this a recent conversation?"

Deena clicked her pen and opened her notebook.

"Oh, heavens. I don't remember. I meant when we were too old and sick to live alone." Millie crossed her arms and pursed her lips, obviously annoyed by Dan's abruptness.

Dan tilted his head toward Deena, throwing the ball to her.

Deena felt a sneeze coming on. Her allergy to cats was infamous. She rubbed her nose. "It sounds like you were a loyal friend to Barbara."

Millie's face tightened. "Barbara was the reason the rest of us stayed here."

"Why is that? Did she ask you to stay?" Deena's eyes began to itch.

"No. She didn't care what the rest of us wanted. You see, there's a man in town who wants to buy up all the property in this area. He held a meeting for all us folks in the neighborhood down at the VFW. Now when was that?" She tapped her chin with her pointer finger. "I think it was in the summer. That's right, because we all wondered why he would give us soup to eat when it was so blasted hot out. Even with those big fans blowing, the sweat was just dripping off of us. Why, Mr.—"

"Hot soup in the summer? That's crazy!" Deena laughed and shook her head.

Dan crossed his legs and brushed cat hair off his pants.

Deena felt it coming. She sneezed. Then sneezed again. "Sorry. Cats."

"Bless you, dear," Millie said and pointed to a box of tissues.

Deena took a few and walked over to stand by the screen door. "You say he gathered the residents for a meeting? What did he offer you?"

"He offered us sixty thousand dollars each for our houses. That's a fortune for some folks. But there was one condition. It was all or nothing. We either all sold and took the money, or it was no deal." She sliced the air with her hand.

Deena held a tissue to her nose, just in case. "Obviously, y'all didn't take the deal. Why not?"

"A bunch of us wanted to. Including me. Sixty thousand dollars is a lot of money. But there were several holdouts. Mainly Barbara." Her voice grew more animated as she spoke. "She was dead set on staying put. Then he upped it to seventy-five thousand! That's when things really got contentious. We even got together and talked it over a few more times, but she wouldn't budge. Said memories were worth more than money."

"You disagree?" Deena asked.

"Before long, I'll probably lose my mind and won't be able to remember the past anyway. That money could have gone a long way toward finding a nice place in a retirement center. Instead, I'm stuck in this old rat trap with a leaky roof and broken pipes."

Dan leaned forward on the couch. "Was this man Marty Fisk, by any chance?"

"Sure was." She rocked back and forth. "After a while, the other people just dropped it. Gave up. That is, until last week."

Dan look up from his notepad. "What happened last week?"

Millie grabbed the arms of the rocker and stared back at Dan. "Well, jiminy crickets! Have you already forgotten that Barbara was killed last week?"

Dan looked sheepish. "I meant—"

"Just two days later, people were jawin' about getting back in touch with that Mr. Fisk and trying to make a deal."

"And are you?" Deena asked.

"You bet I am. But it all depends on Barbara's grandchildren, Katy and Travis. If they sell, then we can, too."

Deena pulled out another clean tissue. "That seems like a lot of pressure for them. Did Mr. Fisk say what he planned to do with the property?"

"Nope. We asked, but he wouldn't say. Seemed kinda fishy. But bad money spends the same as good, you know."

Deena thought of several arguments she could make but just shook her head in agreement.

Dan looked at his notes. "One last question. Have you seen any suspicious vehicles around here lately?"

"You mean besides that red sports car sneaking around here the night Barbara was killed?"

Deena cringed.

"Yeah, besides that," Dan said. "Maybe a van. A white van?"

"I've seen a white van, but then I've seen a lot of trucks and vans. They looked like utility trucks to me. Mostly all from the same company with a big blue sign on the side."

"What company?" Dan asked.

"Jackson Oil and Gas."

Dan made a note and stood up. "Thank you for your time, Mrs. Canfield. You've been very helpful."

"Why, you are most welcome." She walked to the door and patted Deena's arm. "I would invite you to come back any time, but I'm hoping to be long gone myself. Not dead, mind you—just moved."

# Chapter 18

**T**wo missed calls, both from Lloyd Pryor. He was probably looking for her story about Sister Natasha. Deena thought she'd have more luck squirming out of this hot water in person than on the phone.

She and Dan both agreed that Mrs. Canfield seemed somewhat suspicious. Instead of a loyal, caring neighbor, she came across more as an old Grinch ready to take advantage of her neighbor's misfortune. Dan said he would see what the police had on her. He was also going to look into Jackson Oil and Gas. Before he left, Deena gave him the license plate number of the white van so he could ask one of his friends at the DMV to check on it.

Deena's assignment was to talk to Natasha's butler. She hoped he would call this evening. First, however, she wanted to smooth things over with her boss. Hopefully, she could then finally get to her antique booth and unload the boxes from her car.

On her way to the newspaper office, she drove by the psychic's house again just to see how business was going. Sure enough, there were five cars, and several of them had more than one woman inside. She figured Sister Natasha must be pulling in a fortune.

The *Northeast Texas Tribune* distributed their newspapers on Tuesdays, Thursdays, and Saturdays. The afternoons before distribution days were always the most hectic as reporters rushed to meet deadlines, page editors wrote headlines, and everybody proofed for possible errors.

When Deena stood in the doorway of Lloyd's office, she was surprised he shooed out the sports editor and waved her inside.

"I'm working on it," she said, trying to preempt his admonishment.

"Shut the door."

That sounded serious. She swallowed hard. "I went to the psychic reader this morning, but—"

"This isn't about the story," he said. "Actually, that *is* why I called the first time, but now it's about something more important." He pulled up an office chair with his foot and motioned for her to sit. "A phone call came in a few minutes ago from a Mrs. Canfield. She wanted to speak to you. I took the call because everyone else was busy."

She could feel the blood draining from her face. Her mouth felt like sandpaper.

"Seems she wanted to tell you that she saw another one of those trucks you and Dan Carson had asked her about."

Why was he pausing? Just to torture her?

"Have you been working with Dan on his investigation of the Wilde murder?"

She nodded. "Yes." It was all she could manage to say.

He threw his pencil down on the desk. "I'm not going to ask you why you put this newspaper at risk of conflict of interest. I'm not even going to ask you why you would put yourself in the middle of a murder investigation where you were the first suspect." He pushed his chair away from the desk and raised his voice. "But what I am going to ask is why you would go behind my back and disregard a direct order?"

She looked away as "please-officer-don't-give-me-a-ticket" tears poured down her face. She had no excuse. "I didn't know...it was...such a big deal." She grabbed some tissues from his desk and blotted at her face.

"Oh, c'mon now. There's no crying in journalism." He pulled his chair back up to the desk.

"I'm sorry," she said between sniffles. "It's just that Dan asked for my help, and I was excited to do real investigative work."

"I've already talked to Dan. He tried to convince me that I was wasting you on features. But that doesn't change things."

"Does this mean I'm fired?"

Lloyd furrowed his brow, looking like a concerned father. "You know I think a lot of you, but I have no choice. The publisher is already breathing down my neck about another personnel issue."

Her throat tightened. How could she have let this happen? She was a rules follower. Always had been. What would Gary think? Then, one consolation came to mind. "Does this mean I can keep helping Dan?"

Lloyd shook his head in disbelief. "You really do want to be an investigator, don't you?"

She thought about the question, and her answer surprised even herself. "I don't know. What I really want to do, though, is help people. If being an investigator means I can help track down a killer, then that's what I want to do. I guess...I just want to make a difference, as corny as that sounds."

"I get that. That's why I became a journalist." He leaned back in his chair. "Now all I seem to do is try to keep everybody else on staff in line. It's like herding cats."

"Meow," Deena said as she wiped her eyes.

"Maybe you should become a PI. Anyway, you don't work here anymore. You can do anything you want."

She felt her insides settle.

He stood and waved his hand toward the door. "Now get out of here. Clean out your desk. And try to look ashamed."

Deena lowered her head and stifled a grin. As she walked out of the office, she whispered, "Yes, boss."

A million eyes fixed on her as she headed to her desk. She tried to look upset. She grabbed an empty box by the copy machine and began to fill it with personal items. Something nagged at her. What was it? Then the words of the psychic came back to her like a slap in the face. When Deena told Natasha she was a reporter, Sister Natasha had said, "Not for long."

How could she have known? Deena shivered. She felt as if she were being spied on.

The black stapler she had brought from her classroom at Maycroft High School stared at her from the desk drawer. She and that SwingMaster had been through a lot together. Time to go back home. She placed it gingerly inside the box. Was she starting to think like Sandra? Believing objects could have feelings and be haunted? She shook her head to untangle the twisted thoughts.

The bottom desk drawer was stuck, as usual. That's where she kept a sweater for days when the ancient heater would kick off and the old building would drop to sub-zero temperatures.

"Sorry about this."

She looked up to see Dan towering above her desk.

"It's fine," she said, yanking on the drawer and falling back on the floor.

"The thing is, the police just picked up Travis Wilde for the murder of his grandmother. Looks like you lost your job for nothing."

"TRAVIS WILDE? THE GRANDSON?" Gary seemed surprised to hear about the arrest.

They sat at the kitchen table eating the spaghetti and garlic bread Deena had made for dinner. She had timed it so that Gary could test the pasta for doneness as soon as he got home. She had a tendency to over or undercook it. The red wine was already open, and she was almost to the bottom of her glass.

Deena cut her spaghetti. "I guess he's the obvious suspect since he had the most to gain by her death. I just didn't take him for a murderer. A first class jerk, but not a murderer." She sprinkled on an extra dose of parmesan cheese. "But then I guess it's hard for me to imagine anyone being a murderer."

Gary twirled long strands of noodles into his spoon. He took pride in his pasta prowess. "So the guy comes to town, strangles his grandmother, hides out, comes back a few days later, and tries to sell the house?"

"And don't forget that he also contacted the insurance company."

"The guy's got guts, I'll give him that." He stuck the whole fork-full of spaghetti in his mouth.

"I feel a little bad about suspecting Marty Fisk of murder. I still think he's up to something, but at least he's not a killer." Deena looked down and rolled her eyes. Even with cutting her pasta into little pieces, she still managed to drop some on her blouse.

She got up to get a towel to wipe it off. "I'll be curious to find out what evidence they have against him. Just because he had motive, means, and opportunity, it doesn't mean they have enough for a conviction." She dabbed water and dishwashing liquid on her blouse. "By the way, did you set up a golf game with Ned Morrison?"

Gary poured more wine into their glasses. "I told you, I'm not going on a play date just to snoop on one of my co-workers."

Deena plopped down in her chair and gave him her sad puppy face. She stuck out her bottom lip. "How else are we going to find out if he's planning on getting a divorce to marry Katy?"

Gary picked up his glass. "I decided to take the direct approach and talk to him."

Like a scene out of *Carrie*, Deena spewed red wine all over the table. "You didn't! Tell me you didn't ask him if he was having an affair!"

"Of course not," Gary said, blotting the table with his napkin. "I simply asked him about his wife. I asked if they had any big vacation plans this summer."

Deena let out her breath. "And?"

"He told me that they just bought a house by the lake."

"So? That doesn't mean anything. He could be planning to take Katy there after he divorces."

Gary wiped wine off the edge of his plate. "They co-own it with his in-laws. Does that sound like a guy about to get a divorce?"

"No. You're right. That rat. I knew he was using her. Now I just have to figure out a way to tell her." She picked up her plate and carried it to the kitchen.

"You'll leave me out of it, right?"

"Of course. I can't believe you asked me that."

"Sorry. I trust you." He picked up the rest of the dishes and put them in the kitchen sink. "You cooked. I'll clean."

Deena carried her glass to the counter and sat on a barstool. She twisted back and forth, thinking of the best way to tell Gary her news. Finally, she spit it out. "Speaking of trust, I talked to Lloyd today. He found out I was helping Dan."

Gary looked back over his shoulder and waited.

"It seems that it's a violation of office policy to go against your boss' orders." She scrunched her nose. "I got fired." There. She'd said it.

"Fired? Again?"

"Now wait. Technically I quit my teaching job, remember? Besides, I wasn't going to be happy writing about the Junior League and Sunday socials."

"I know, but what are you going to do now?" He rinsed off the plates and put them in the dishwasher. "Take up baking? Gardening? Read to the blind?

"They have audio books for the blind now. Anyway, I still have my antique business."

Gary cut his eyes at her. "It's not much of a business when the stuff's just sitting in your car."

"Ouch," she said. "I guess I deserve that."

Her cell phone rang. It was Dan. What he told her came as a surprise. She promised to call him back if she heard from Natasha's butler.

"What was that all about?" Gary asked.

"It turns out that Dan's source at the police department jumped the gun. Travis Wilde was arrested for skipping out on his bail in Harris County, not for murder. The police are going to hold him as long as possible while they look for more evidence and check out his alibi for Tuesday night."

"So they must think he's guilty."

"I'm sure. I can't wait to see what happens next. For now, I want to keep helping Dan, for Katy's sake. As for another job, I'm sure something else will eventually come along. You said we didn't need the money, especially the little bit I was making part-time at the newspaper."

Gary hung the dishtowel on the hook, making sure it was perfectly centered. "You're right. But you're still a young woman. I don't want you sitting around in a rocking chair knitting scarves all day."

"Like Mrs. Wilde?"

"Believe me," he said, wrapping his arms around her, "you are nothing like Mrs. Wilde. At least, not yet."

She walked over to the patio door to let Hurley outside. The sky had dried up and a bright orange sunset dipped toward the horizon. Reality was finally sinking in. She was now, Deena Sharpe: ex-newspaper reporter.

Sure, she was anxious to help Katy get away from Ned. She might even be able to help Dan uncover some dirt on Marty Fisk. But then what? Maybe after some time passed, Lloyd would hire her back.

Not likely. She blinked back the tears that threatened to emerge. Perhaps the person who really needed help was her.

# Chapter 19

Finding out Travis had been arrested again sent Katy into a tailspin. So much so, she even called in sick from work. It seemed like she and her brother had been cut from different cloths. All she wanted was to find true love. All he wanted was to find a pot of gold.

She had stayed the night again at her grandmother's house, not trusting what Travis might do or take. She heard him come in late. At least she had assumed he was the source of the racket that caused her to bolt up straight in the bed. Either he made the noise, or the place was haunted. Even Mrs. Canfield's dog came to life and barked at all the strange sounds.

He was gone when she got up in the morning. Apparently, he went to meet Charla Hicks at her real estate office. That's where the police picked him up. That tacky woman even had the gall to phone Katy and ask if she'd re-considered the offer on the house. Katy made it crystal clear that she had no intention of selling. Not now. Not ever.

A public defender from the firm of Lyons and Sons was assigned to Travis' case. The judge refused to set bail since he was obviously a flight risk.

This was by no means Travis' first brush with the law. He'd been picked up for writing bad checks and loan fraud on several occasions. Their grandmother had given him more money than Katy cared to think about. Why wouldn't he just get a job and work like everyone else?

She continued to putter around the house filling boxes and sorting through her grandmother's papers. The will she found said her grandmother's estate would be divided evenly between herself and Travis. She didn't have a clue what to do with the will. A guy from the bar had recently dealt with the death of his father. She would ask him what to do.

In the meantime, she started making the place a little more her own. She'd given notice the day before to her apartment manager that she'd be moving out at the end of the month. Having heard about her grandmother's death, he agreed to return her security deposit even though she was breaking her lease. She'd been sleeping in her old bedroom, but the window had leaked, leaving behind a mildew odor. Tonight, she would sleep in her grandmother's room.

She looked in the refrigerator hoping that new food would have magically appeared. Usually, she'd eat dinner at the bar. The staff would pool their money and someone would pick up fried chicken or barbeque sandwiches or pizza. What she wouldn't give for a hot slice of pepperoni right now.

Instead, she pulled out a loaf of bread and made a peanut butter and jelly sandwich from fixings she had brought over from her apartment. At least she had brewed a fresh pitcher of iced tea. She pulled it out of the refrigerator and opened the freezer for ice. A stack of foil wrapped packages covered in ice crystals toppled over as she pulled out the tray.

Trash pickup was tomorrow. If she threw these out today, they wouldn't rot in the garbage can all week. She pulled up the kitchen can and started filling it with mystery food. The refrigerator was almost as bad. She checked the dates on the bottles of salad dressing and pickles. Some were more than a year old. She tossed them into the can. By the time she finished, the bag was so full she feared it would tear. She remembered seeing a box of leaf bags in the carport. She went out the back door.

The sun was setting and casting long shadows on the yard. The once vibrant lawn had mostly gone to seed. There were deep tracks in the mud where Travis had been parking his car behind the house. She looked around in the carport for the bags.

Rusty tools lay everywhere. If she were going to live there, she wanted to plant a vegetable garden. She scooted grimy boxes and tubs around on the shelves to get an idea of what tools were there. Something caught her eye. It was Gran's old sunhat and garden gloves.

Tears streamed down her face as she remembered the days she spent working in the yard by her grandmother's side. She had discovered later that her grandmother never cared much for gardening, but she had done it with Katy as a sort of distraction. Something to take her mind off the grief of losing her parents.

The memories flooded her thoughts as she opened the back screen door. She spotted the trashcan and remembered the leaf bags she had forgotten to retrieve. A rustling noise in the front room drew her attention. It sounded bigger than Mrs. Canfield's cat sneaking in through the open window. "Hello? Is someone there?" Had someone been at her front door?

Her heart beat faster as she picked up the baseball bat from the corner of the kitchen. She inched toward the dining room. Suddenly, the sound was behind her at the back kitchen door. She swung around and raised the wooden bat above her head. Bringing it down with all her might, she hit nothing but air. Then she felt a booming pain on the back of her head. She dropped and landed face down on the ground.

She didn't hear the crackling of glass. She didn't see the shadowy figure. She didn't know if she would live or die.

# Chapter 20

**R**oscoe stared at Deena Sharpe's business card. He wanted to call her, but maybe now wasn't the right time. Business had been good ever since word got out that Tonya had used her gift to find that kid.

Gift. Her biggest gift was him. And if she didn't quit nagging him about his late night errands, she'd be packing her bags and riding a Greyhound straight back to Vegas.

Along with the money he had hidden from her, they had made plenty to pay for their fake IDs and travel to Mexico. It was just hard to walk away from this honey hole. Especially now that he was earning his secret stash. One month. By that time, they'd have enough cash to get there and live high on the hog for at least a year.

He looked at Tonya lying in the bed. Her breathing had steadied. She was asleep. Now he just needed to get out of the house without waking her up. He left the television volume on low. It would drown out some of the noise he might make opening and closing their creaky front door.

He tip-toed down the front porch and walked around to the back of the house, looking through the window to see if she had woken up and turned on a light. Nothing. He headed for his car.

He drove a few blocks to the drop-off point behind the pawn shop and checked his cell phone for the time. He was early. A few beers from the convenience store would make the time pass quicker.

The rain had stopped and a bright moon lit up the wet roads. He worried it might be harder to keep from being seen with all the light. He pulled up to the store and waited for another car to drive off. Inside, he pulled two bottles out of the cooler. As he set them on the counter, he noticed a rack of t-shirts. He chose a black one with a Texas flag on the front. The dark shirt would work better than the pale blue one he was wearing.

He drove to the back of the pawn shop and waited. He flipped through the radio stations but could only find country music. The CDs in the glove compartment were already in the car when they bought it somewhere in Nevada. He put one in the player and turned up the volume. As soon as it began playing, he fumbled to find the eject button. Holding the disc by the window, he read the label by the light of the moon. Christmas Classics? He hurled it out of the car like a Frisbee.

The other CD wasn't much better, but it beat listening to country music on the radio. For the next half hour, he lay back in the seat with his eyes closed listening to the sweet sounds of Sinatra.

When the CD began to skip, he opened his eyes. He checked the time again. Why wasn't he here yet? He waited another twenty minutes, jumping at every howl of the wind, crackle of a tree branch, and crunch of tires as cars drove past.

Finally, he decided he'd waited long enough. He found the number in his phone and called it. After four rings, it went to voicemail. He didn't want to leave a message, so he looked around the parking lot wondering what to do. If he did nothing, he wouldn't get paid. Maybe he should improvise.

He was just about to pull out of the parking lot when the phone rang. He told the caller, "I'm here. Where are you?"

The voice on the other end was gravelly and angry. Roscoe clenched his jaw as Marty Fisk gave him a good chewing out.

"But—" Roscoe tried to defend himself, but the caller wouldn't listen.

"Yes, sir," he said at last and ended the call. He threw down his phone on the seat and got out of the car. He couldn't believe Marty Fisk had just called him an idiot. The man had never said the box would be in the dumpster.

Roscoe stared at the filthy metal container and then went back to the car to get his gloves and blue shirt. No way was he touching that disgusting mess with his bare hands. He pushed open the lid and heard the scuttling sound of mice or rats or worse. He pulled up on the leg of his jeans so he could get his foot high enough to step on the crossbar. He hoisted himself up and was assaulted by an ungodly stench.

He spotted the shoebox right where it was supposed to be. He threw his blue shirt over the top of it and lifted it out slowly, hoping that the rubber bands keeping it shut wouldn't break. As he jumped down to the ground, he heard chirping and fluttering. How many of those things did he put in here?

Roscoe couldn't get the cardboard box in the trunk fast enough for his liking. He closed the trunk lid and shuddered. As he jumped back in the car and drove to the Wildes' house, he thought about poor Katy. Besides being a knock-out, she seemed like a sweet kid. He hated to do this to her, but money was money. The nightly haunts were supposed to make her want to sell the house. Fisk had tried the same thing with the grandmother, but it didn't work.

He parked in the same spot as he had the night before, on the block behind hers and down in front of a vacant lot. He cut through the brush and came up to the rear of the house carrying the box still wrapped in his shirt. The lights were off, but her car was there. She must be asleep. He jiggled the kitchen window and the lock fell loose. Slowly, he slid open the window and waited. No noise. No lights.

He would have to reach up high above his head to open the box and release its contents inside the house. Then he would shut the window as quick as he could to keep the nasty varmints from flying out.

He took a deep breath. The box vibrated in his hands as he pulled off the rubber band. He held the lid on tight as he felt the contents pushing against it, trying to escape.

The chirping grew louder. He reached as high as he could and leaned in so that the box was through the window. One. Two. Three! He pulled back the lid and a swarm of brown bats flew out the window and blanketed his face. Gritting his teeth to keep from yelling, he swatted them off as he dove for the ground. He lay in a fetal position for a full minute before he had the guts to open his eyes.

And just like that, they were gone.

Instead of staying in the house to scare Katy, they had flown toward a streetlight and disappeared. He stood up, brushing mud and leaves from his pants. Now what? Fisk probably wouldn't even pay him for this one.

Then it occurred to him. How would Fisk know the bats never made it inside? He'd show him the empty box and tell him it all went as planned. Cha-ching!

He looked around on the ground. There was the lid, but where was the box? He must have dropped it inside. He heard a car coming and plastered himself against the back of the house. A nearby dog barked, but soon settled down.

He would need to go back in through the window and retrieve the box. That was all there was to it. Maybe the window was over the kitchen sink, and he could just reach in and pick it up.

The window was too high for him to pull himself up. He looked around for something to stand on, spotting a stack of cement blocks next to the carport. He carried back two of the blocks and stacked one on the other. He stepped up on top to test their sturdiness, rocking sideways. This would have to do.

The window had slipped down a bit so he raised it as high as it would go. He heaved himself up with his arms and lunged his body forward, teeter-tottering on the window ledge. It was dark inside except for moonlight from the windows. He looked down, hoping to see the box.

He was right. The kitchen sink was below him, but the box wasn't there. It had fallen on the floor and had slid under a small table. He leaned in further and blinked his eyes. Off to his left he saw something sparkling like a swarm of fireflies. Half inside, half out, he held onto the faucet to steady himself. When he looked again, he realized what it was. Katy's body, covered with broken glass, was lying lifeless on the floor.

The shock caused him to pitch backward and crack his head against the window sill. Shattered glass fell all over him. One large piece sliced his arm, and he cried out in pain. The cement block under his feet fell off to the side.

For a moment, he thought he was stuck, his legs flailing. When he pushed himself up with his hands, bits of glass pierced his skin. He ducked his head as he fell back to the ground. His ears rang and a barking sound grew louder until it thundered just above him.

"Help! Help! Call 9-1-1!" A woman with a flashlight pulled on the dog's leash, trying to back away.

He got up and ran back through the brush and to his car. He jammed a bloody hand into his pocket to pull out his keys. His hands shook as he tried to open the lock. When he jumped inside and turned on the car, he left the headlights off. As he pulled away, he hit a metal trash can sitting by the curb, sending it flying. The sirens grew louder as he sped to the end of the street. There was only one way out of the neighborhood, and lights were flashing in that direction.

It was now or never. He floored it toward a vacant lot. The old sedan hit the tall curb, throwing Roscoe into the steering wheel. Another jolt rocked him backward as the car smashed to the ground. The engine sputtered and died.

Like the swarm of bats that had attacked him just minutes early, within seconds he was surrounded again. This time it was by the police.

# Chapter 21

**B**arking dogs again. Deena still hadn't remembered to change her ringtone for callers who weren't family. She grabbed the cell phone from her nightstand and glanced at the time. It was almost two in the morning. Dan? Why would he be calling her at this hour?

"Sorry to bother you, but I thought you'd want to know. Your girl Katy is in the hospital. They caught the guy who did it."

Deena felt her stomach dive into her intestines. "What happened? Who did it?"

"They haven't released his name yet. Looks like he hit her over the head with a glass pitcher. She's alive but unconscious."

Deena felt like screaming. She wanted to throw something. How could this have happened? She wanted to blame Dan but knew he was just the messenger. She wiped tears from her cheek. "Can I see her?"

"Not yet. Maybe tomorrow. I'm sorry, hon, maybe I should have waited to call in the morning."

"No. I'm glad you did."

"We should have more details in the morning. Call me later when you're up."

She sat back and leaned against the headboard. It felt like a weird nightmare. The kind where you try to run away, but your feet just won't move.

She sunk back down under the covers and closed her eyes. There were so many questions she hadn't thought to ask Dan. Like, where was Katy when the attack happened? At home or at work? How did they catch the guy? Was the attack related to Mrs. Wilde's death? She knew the morning would bring more answers. All she wanted to do now was sleep, but there was little chance of that happening.

THE SOUND OF GARY TURNING on the shower startled Deena awake. She must have finally drifted off to sleep. Stumbling out of bed, she walked to the mirror in the small dressing area of the bedroom. She looked as bad as she felt. Her head boomed from a lack of sleep, and dark circles engulfed her eyes. Coffee was the only possible cure for what was going on in her fuzzy brain.

Just as she reached the kitchen, her cell phone rang in the bedroom. She debated just letting it go to voicemail, but then thought that it might be Dan. She ran back and dove across the bed to reach it before the last bark. "Ian? What's up? Is it Sandra?"

"No. She's good. It's you."

"What do you mean?"

"I just got assigned a new case from the county. My client has allegedly attacked someone. What I want to know is why your business card was in his pocket?"

# Chapter 22

Not knowing what to expect, Deena entered the Perry County Jail on Tuesday morning with cautious anticipation. It felt a lot like going to the dentist. She knew she needed to be there but would have preferred being anywhere else on earth.

She called Ian from the lobby to let him know she had arrived. A buzzer sounded and the door opened. A man she recognized from church led her back to the visitation area.

It looked a lot like the DMV. Several rows of chairs were lined up in the middle of the room. The front wall had four glassed-in cubbies with telephones. A thirty-something guy wearing an orange jumpsuit leaned on his elbow. He was talking to a woman with graying hair.

Ian sat at a small table in the corner, scribbling notes. A tiny tape recorder lay on the edge of the table.

He glanced up. "Good, you're here. Have a seat."

The blank walls, mounted security camera, and tape recorder felt intimidating. Although the room was cool, her palms began to sweat.

"Am I being questioned on the record? I mean, officially?"

Ian pushed back his shaggy dark bangs. "Well, yes."

"Should I call my lawyer?"

Ian laughed.

She didn't mean it to be funny. She had to testify back in December in her legal case, and she was having flashbacks. Of course, that time, Ian was on *her* side.

"I see you're nervous. I'm just going to ask you a couple of simple questions on the record. That's all. You don't have to answer if you don't want to."

This was her best friend's husband. She knew she could trust him. After a quick cleansing breath, she said, "Proceed, counselor."

"Mrs. Sharpe, have you ever met Roscoe Trainor?"

"Roscoe? Is that the guy dressed like a butler at Sister Natasha's house?"

Ian nodded.

"Yes. Yesterday."

He held up his hand for her to wait for the next question. "How did he get your business card?"

She had learned from her previous deposition that less was more. She chose her words carefully. "I went to the house to have Sister Natasha give me a reading and to see if I could interview her for a story for the newspaper. She asked me—*ordered* me, to leave. Mr. Trainor asked me to leave my card in the box on the front porch and said that he would call me. So I did." She was satisfied with her answer.

Ian took notes as she spoke. "And did you write the story?"

"No," she said abruptly.

"Will you be writing the story in the future?"

"No."

He looked up from his notes. "Why not?"

"I got fired yesterday."

He reached over and shut off the tape recorder. "What on earth happened?"

She braced herself for another tongue-lashing. "Lloyd Pryor changed my assignment. He told me to stay away from the murder investigation and the story about Councilman Fisk. I told you about that, remember?"

"Yes. And...?"

"I didn't stay away. I've been helping Dan Carson interview some leads. Pryor found out and...*eek*." She drug her thumb across the front of her throat. "I got the axe."

"Deena. I told you—"

"I know. I've heard it all."

Ian closed his notepad. "So, what have you found out?"

She crossed her arms, surprised by the question. "Are you asking as my friend or my lawyer? Or as that horrible man's attorney?"

"All three."

She didn't like his answer and wasn't sure how much she should say. "Without giving any specifics, I think Marty Fisk is up to no good. I think Barbara and Katy Wilde are connected to him somehow."

Ian tapped his pen on the table. "What does Gary think? About your going rogue, that is."

"He's on board, as long as I keep out of harm's way."

"In order to defend my client, I need to know what you know. I don't have time for a lot of leg work. Sounds like you and Dan have a head start on this thing."

Deena shook her head. "I know it's your job, but how can you defend such a despicable criminal?"

"Shall I quote the constitution or do you want the short version? I think Roscoe Trainor is innocent."

"Innocent? From the little I've heard, he was caught red-handed!"

"Things aren't always what they seem. You know that."

Like in a cartoon, she could practically see the wheels turning in Ian's head. At last, he spit it out.

"What if I hire you to work for me as an investigator? I can pay you a modest salary. You can help me dig out the truth, whatever that turns out to be."

It was Deena's turn for a lightbulb moment. Before he could change his mind, she answered with a resounding, "Yes!"

Now she just had to convince Gary and Dan it was a good idea.

Her cell phone barked in her pocket.

"You need to change that ringtone if you're going to be taken seriously in this business."

She nodded. "Hello?"

It was Dan. He said he had some new information. When he asked her to meet him at the hospital, she jumped on it. After all, she needed to talk to him in person, not knowing how he would feel about sharing his notes with a defense attorney.

THE MAYCROFT REGIONAL Hospital was well staffed, despite its small size. Within those walls, babies were born, bones were set, and bodies were brought in before being shuffled off to the funeral home.

Deena glanced around the reception area.

Dan was leaning against the reception desk talking to a clerk, perhaps another one of his contacts. He waved a salute before walking up to Deena. "She's still in ICU, but the doctor said she's stable."

"Can we see her?"

"Only you can." He led the way to a waiting area. "I talked to Dr. Shultz and explained the situation. He knew about her grandmother, but he didn't know her only other relative—her brother Travis—was in jail. He agreed you could go in to see her for a few minutes."

"Is she still unconscious?" Deena wrung her hands. "Is there anything I need to do?"

"Nah. Just tell her you're here. You women seem to know what to say."

"Right. But before I go back there, I need to tell you what just happened."

Dan pulled out his notepad. "I got something, too."

They moved away from an older couple who were filling out forms.

"You go first," Deena said.

"Jackson Oil and Gas. The company listed on the trucks Mrs. Canfield saw. They're not a utility company. They dig oil wells. It turns out there's oil in them thar hills."

"You mean the neighborhood Fisk wants to buy?"

"I checked the property records. He already owns several houses and vacant lots there. There was information about old mineral rights. My guess is he realized there could be oil or natural gas underneath and hired Jackson Oil to do some testing."

"That explains what Georgia Parks said. That Fisk wasn't planning to build on the land." Deena's eyes narrowed. "That means he only wanted the area re-zoned so he could force the owners to sell their property. What a creep."

Dan nodded. "That's right. It also makes the land a lot more valuable. He obviously had been keeping that information secret to avoid competition for the property."

"So why would he tell his mistress if it was such a big secret?"

"Georgia is a gold digger. I wouldn't be surprised if she were the brains behind his brawn."

"But wouldn't the city or county have to give him permission to drill? Even if the area were re-zoned, he'd still have to get the okay."

"Maybe he had a two-step plan. First, buy the property under the pretense of revitalizing the city, and then request to drill the oil underneath. There's plenty of private wells around here."

"But, he couldn't do anything until he got his hands on the land. And Barbara Wilde was the only one standing in his way." Her throat tightened. "And then Katy."

Dan sighed. "I know. So, where does the brother, Travis, come in?"

"Maybe Fisk paid him." Deena couldn't believe she was back to suspecting the city councilman of murder. "It seems like a lot of people stood to benefit from Mrs. Wilde's death. Travis with the life insurance and selling the house, Mrs. Canfield and the other neighbors, and Marty Fisk."

"Greed. It's at the heart of most murders."

"But Travis was in jail when his sister was attacked."

Dan shook his head. "That's going to be a big problem for the police. Although it's possible the two attacks weren't connected, it seems unlikely."

Deena frowned. "I think we should tell the police our theory...and Ian."

"Ian Davis? The defense attorney?" He tilted his head. "Why?"

"Because he's my new boss. As of about thirty minutes ago."

"You know, you could have led with that piece of information."

Deena pulled Ian's business card from her purse and handed it to Dan. "I know you don't always trust lawyers, but Ian wants to find the truth. He's been assigned to represent Roscoe Trainor, the man arrested for attacking Katy. I'll know more when I meet with Ian again this afternoon."

Dan sat back and shut his eyes. "Is he paying you at least?"

"Ian? Yes."

"This goes against my better judgement, but it seems like we all want the same thing." He sat up to look Deena straight in the eyes. "You know that if this Roscoe fella turns out to be guilty of attacking Katy, Ian is still going to defend him."

"I know." The bats in her belly fluttered again. "I guess I'll cross that ditch when I come to it." She put her hand on his arm. "Will you help us?"

He nodded in agreement. "But it's got to be a two-way street. If you guys get a tip, I need to know about it."

"I think Ian would agree to that."

"I need to head to the office. I've got some calls to make so I can file this story about the attack and arrest. I sure wish I knew if Fisk had an alibi for last night." He stuck the card and his notepad back in his shirt pocket. "You do realize that when you give our information about Fisk to Ian, he'll be on the phone to the cops quicker than liquor."

"Is that bad?"

"I suppose not. Based on what Mrs. Canfield told us about the buyout and this new info about the oil, it's probably time the police figure out what Fisk's involvement is."

"And Mrs. Canfield's," Deena added.

"Right. You go check on Katy, and I'll go write this story about Roscoe Trainor. I'll call you later."

They stood up and Deena patted his back. "Just the facts, Dan. Our client may be innocent."

When Dan left, Deena went up to the desk and gave her name to the clerk who directed her to the ICU. Deena was well aware of its location, having spent several days there the past winter.

One of Deena's former students was at the nurses' station. She led Deena back to see Katy.

Monitors and tubes took up most of the space in the curtained-off area where Katy lay. If not for the steady beeping sound, Deena might have thought she was dead. A white bandage around her thick brown hair covered what Deena assumed was a head full of stitches. There were several scratches and cuts on her arms and hands. She also had stitches on one of her cheeks. The cuts were obviously due to the shattered glass pitcher.

Deena stood next to the bed and put her hand softly over Katy's, carefully avoiding the IV tubes. "Katy. It's Deena Sharpe. I'm here." She wasn't sure if the girl could hear her, but it didn't matter. There were things Deena needed to say. "I am so sorry this happened to you, but you're going to be okay. I'm going to find out who did this to you. I'm going to find out what happened to your grandmother." The monitor continued its steady pace. "You don't worry about anything except getting better. I'll be back to see you soon."

She reached over and ran her fingers lightly across Katy's cheek. She looked so young and helpless. As Deena left the hospital room, no tears fell from her eyes. She was more determined than ever to find justice for Barbara and Katy Wilde.

BY LUCK, GARY ANSWERED the phone when Deena called. It was only March, but for a tax accountant and financial advisor, every day in spring was like April 14. She had promised to call him after meeting with Ian. She sat in the parking lot in front of the antique mall, waiting for Sandra. She had agreed to close the thrift shop for an hour to help Deena with her booth as long as they could pick up croissants and lattes from the Coffee Hut after.

"Whatcha got?" Gary asked as though he were waiting for a stock tip. Deena was used to his businessman-persona when she called him at the office.

"Good news and bad news. The good news is that I have a new job."

"Already? That's great!"

"The bad news is that I'm working for Ian Davis as an investigator into the Marty Fisk matter and the attack on Katy." She waited. She could hear heavy breathing.

"If that's what you want to do, I think it's fine. Just stay out of trouble and don't get hurt."

"Wow. That was easier than I thought."

"I've learned that you're going to do whatever you want anyway, so I might as well be supportive."

"Thank you, my love." She smacked a kiss into the phone. "I'll see you at dinner."

For the first time that day, she relaxed. Maybe things were turning around.

Sandra pulled up next to Deena's SUV and got out. "Isn't that the same stuff you had in your car last week?"

"Yes. I've been busy."

"It sounds like you're going to get busier from what I hear. I talked to Ian."

Deena lifted the back hatch, and they each picked up a box. "How do you feel about that?"

"I think it's good," Sandra said, holding the front door open with her foot. "He has a hard time keeping dependable, trustworthy people in his office."

Janet was behind the counter. "Hey you two. Long time no see."

Deena nodded. "Got a bunch of stuff to put out today."

They walked back to Deena's booth. She didn't care that the space was dusty and needed to be swept. She set down the box and put her hands on her hips. "Ugh. Where to start?"

"I'll get a dolly and bring in more boxes. You put things where you want them on the shelves."

Deena pulled out vases, dishes, and pottery, setting them anywhere they would go. This was the one place where she was usually meticulous, staging items in vignettes to give them a homey appeal. She needed to make short work of this task so she could get to Ian's office on time.

After Sandra's second load, she stopped to catch her breath. "Looks like you've been busy shopping, girlfriend."

"And this isn't all of it. I still have more back at the house."

"It doesn't really do you any good if you don't have it out in front of your customers."

Deena rolled her eyes. "Thanks, Gary."

Sandra laughed, but quickly turned serious. She put her hand on Deena's arm. "You know, I just want to warn you about something. I'd hate to see you have a big letdown. Most of the people Ian defends are guilty. This guy who was arrested for attacking that girl, he's probably guilty, too."

Deena shook her head. "But Ian said he thinks he's innocent."

"Ian thinks everybody's innocent. That's why he's a defense attorney."

Deena frowned, looking down at the dirty floor.

Sandra moved the dolly out of the way. "I'm just saying, they arrested one guy for killing his grandmother and another for attacking that girl. They will likely both be convicted and everything else will just work itself out. Just thought you should get a reality check." She headed back to the parking lot.

A reality check? That was ironic coming from the person who thought her storeroom was haunted. In this instance though, Sandra made a lot of sense. It definitely knocked the wind from her sails, but Deena didn't want to give up. She remembered her promise to Katy. If Roscoe Trainor were guilty, she'd help prove it. As far as defending him in court, that would be left in Ian's hands.

# Chapter 23

The law office of Ian Davis was in an old Victorian house in desperate need of refurbishing. He had planned to hire a contractor but just hadn't found the time. Peeling paint and crooked columns made it look more like a fixer upper than a professional law office. A musty smell, like an old lady's closet, assaulted Deena's nose when she opened the front door.

She stepped into a foyer that led to a wide stairway. A rope had been tied across the staircase to block entry. There was a hand-written sign warning visitors to keep out of that area. Not exactly the most welcoming of offices. To the left was a dining area and kitchen. To the right was a large room that was probably once a parlor. It had been partitioned off with freestanding walls and had an assortment of old desks and tables.

A young girl with a blond bob talked on the phone while taking notes. Ian stood by an old-style desktop copier with an inch-thick stack of papers. A preppy looking twenty-something wearing a button-down shirt, jeans, and tennis shoes, got up from his desk and walked up to greet her. "Can I help you?" he asked politely.

"I'm Deena Sharpe."

Ian stopped what he was doing. "Hey, Deena. This is Rob. He's the office manager and a paralegal."

They shook hands.

"That's Amy," Ian said, pointing to the girl on the phone. "She's also a paralegal."

Amy looked up from her notes and waved her pencil.

"Deena is going to be doing some investigative work for us."

"Welcome," Rob said. "We could use all the help we can get."

"Let's go into my office." Ian headed to the only area in the room with four walls.

As she followed him, she tried to take in as much of the space as possible. This was definitely not what she expected. Ian's previous office was in a swank part of town. There, the waiting area had been professionally decorated, and Ian's office was large enough to host a small party. She didn't recall having smelled an odor there.

She was obviously the oldest person in the office. She could probably be Amy's mother. What was she getting herself into?

"Have a seat. I trust you talked to Dan Carson. Is he okay with our arrangement?"

"Yes," she said, settling into a chrome office chair covered in worn, fake leather. "As long as we keep him in the loop, too."

"As long as it's in the best interest of our client, we'll tell him everything we know."

"Sounds fair."

"So I talked to Roscoe this morning, and he gave me an earful." Ian stood up and yelled over the temporary wall. "Hey Rob. Can you finish making those copies?" He sat back down and reached into his bottom desk drawer, pulling out a blank legal pad. He set a pen on top and slid it across the desk to Deena.

"The police think Miss Wilde was attacked around seven o'clock, just before sunset, based on the condition she was in when they got there. Roscoe claims he was at home with Tonya Webber. That's her real name. She's the psychic—and his girlfriend. They moved here from Las Vegas and set up shop. He has an outstanding warrant for his arrest."

Deena looked up from taking notes.

"For pick-pocketing. But, since he's proven to be a flight risk, the judge denied bail. To be honest, I feel better with him behind bars. That way he can't do anything stupid."

She wrote as fast as she could, feeling like she'd just opened Pandora's Box and a whole bunch of new characters popped out.

"So Sister Natasha is his alibi?"

"Yes, pretty thin, don't you think?"

"More like *medium*. Because she's a psychic..." She bit her lip.

"I got it." He tapped his pen on the desk. "You know that Sandra has bought that psychic's shtick hook, line, and sinker. What do *you* think?"

"I'm on the fence. Did you ask Roscoe about her?"

"He's being tight-lipped about the business. I didn't push him on it for now. I was more interested in what he said about Marty Fisk. Says he was doing a job for him last night. That's why he was at Miss Wilde's house. Seems Fisk has paid him to scare her. Trying to get her to sell her house."

"Poor Katy."

"Miss Wilde. That's how we need to refer to her since we are defending Roscoe. It makes her seem less sympathetic."

She had a lot to learn. "So what did he say he was doing there last night?"

"Get this. Fisk paid him to release bats in the house. Says he looked inside, and she was already on the ground. He thought she was dead and ran off. A neighbor called the police, and they picked him up trying to get away."

Ian went on to explain how Roscoe got the bats at the back of the pawn shop and took them over to the house. The police had the shoebox, and there were definite signs of it having held the bats. But since Roscoe was wearing gloves, there were no fingerprints. Ian told her about the blood on the windowsill and on Roscoe. The police were waiting to see if any of it belonged to the victim. The fact that he was covered in glass and that she had been hit on the head with an iced tea pitcher, didn't look good for his case.

"So if the assault occurred at seven and he was arrested at around midnight, how do the police explain the discrepancy?"

"For now, they don't have to explain anything. They're just gathering evidence. They will likely say he was going back to finish the job or cover his tracks."

Ian twisted back and forth in his swivel chair, just the way Lloyd Pryor did when he was thinking. "I guess you can see why it's important to know what's going on with Councilman Fisk."

Deena cleared her throat. "Here's what I know."

Now Ian became the note-taker.

She told him about the meeting with the homeowners and his offer to buy their property.

"All or nothing? That's unusual," Ian said.

She went on to tell him about the re-zoning proposals and Jackson Oil and Gas. She also told him about the real estate agent and the latest offer to buy Katy's house. Finally, she mentioned the insurance policy and Travis Wilde.

"I'm not sure it's a smart legal tactic to tie the murder case and the assault charge together. But from an outsider's standpoint, it seems all roads point to Marty Fisk. However, if I were Travis' attorney, I'd definitely be looking at all those other residents. You say there's six or seven? Who's to say one of them wasn't tired of waiting for Mrs. Wilde to die or change her mind? Then when they found out Miss Wilde was stonewalling, they went after her, too."

"Dan and I talked to Mrs. Canfield. She definitely had a motive and the opportunity since she lives right next door to the Wildes. For that matter, I guess the realtor, Charla Hicks, could be a suspect, too. If she were brokering those deals, she stood to make a sizable chunk of change."

Ian grinned and waved his pen toward Deena. "Now you're thinking."

"Is it a big deal that Katy—Miss Wilde—was dating a married man?"

"Of course it is. The man might have wanted to cover up the affair, or his wife could have found out about them. Jealousy and greed are two strong motives. What's his name?"

Deena wished she had kept her mouth closed. Gary had already cleared Ned, and she'd promised Katy she wouldn't say anything. Still, she had never thought about it in the way Ian had put it.

Ian seemed to sense her hesitation. "Don't worry, this isn't a witch hunt. Don't you want to get to the truth? The police will find out anyway. Believe me, affairs are usually the first things they uncover."

Deena thought about Marty Fisk. Dan had easily figured out that Marty was cheating on his wife with Georgia Parks. "I suppose you're right. His name is Ned Garrison."

Ian looked up again. "I know Ned. He used to do my taxes. It's always the quiet ones." He made a note. "I'm going to talk to Detective Evans. He needs to look into Fisk's business dealings. See if he has an alibi for these two crimes. I also need to talk to Roscoe to see if he knows more about Fisk than he's saying. You should be there, too. Do you want to look at the crime scene photos?"

She flinched. "Not yet."

"I get it. We'll meet at the jail at nine in the morning. Okay?"

"Sure." She stood up, holding the notepad against her chest. "Just one thing. Why would the police bother to investigate Fisk now? They've got their man...both of them?"

"That's where we come in. We raise the questions. If they are compelling enough, the police will follow up. The DA's office is a pretty good bunch. Nobody wants to see an innocent person go to prison."

That's how Deena felt, too. But in this case, it seemed like everybody was guilty of *something*.

# Chapter 24

**D**eena tapped her foot nervously Wednesday morning, waiting with Ian for the guard to bring in Roscoe Trainor. The small office was used for attorneys to meet with their clients.

"We need to get you some business cards," Ian had said when they went through security.

It seemed funny that things were moving so fast. Conventional wisdom was that the wheels of justice turned slowly.

The guard opened the door and led Roscoe inside. He was wearing the full criminal get-up, including an orange jumpsuit, leg chains, and handcuffs. Both of his hands were wrapped in gauze and there was a bandage on his face where he had gotten stitches.

Ian motioned toward the leg restraints. "Are these really necessary?"

"You know the rules," the guard said. He pushed Roscoe down into a chair. "I'll be right outside."

Ian waited for the guard to leave. "Roscoe Trainor, this is Deena Sharpe. She's going to be assisting me."

"Hello." She reached out her hand to shake, but pulled it back quickly when she saw the handcuffs. Oops. Another felony faux pas.

"I know you," Roscoe said. "You're that reporter."

"Was a reporter," Deena said. "Now I'm working for Mr. Davis."

"Are you doing okay?" Ian asked. "Do you need anything?"

"Other than getting out of here, not really."

"I'm doing my best," Ian said. "I wanted to ask you a few more questions about Martin Fisk. You said he rented the house you and Miss Webber are living in. When did he first contact you about working for him?"

"It was about a week ago. I was...at the bank. He saw me and said he wanted me to do a couple of jobs for him."

Deena took notes. Ian asked the questions.

"Tell me about those jobs," Ian said.

"First, he wanted me to go to the bar and talk to that girl. See if she was planning on moving into her grandmother's house."

"Did he tell you anything about Mrs. Wilde? About how she died?"

"Absolutely not. I probably wouldn't have agreed to help him if I'd known that."

"Did he tell you why he wanted to know her plans?"

"No. Not that day. A few days later, he called and wanted me to go over to her house and spook her. I asked why. He said he was trying to get her to sell the house."

"What did you do?"

"I went over late that night—on Sunday— and banged around on the outside of the house. Wanted it to sound like a burglar or a ghost."

Deena was starting to get a picture of the real Roscoe Trainor. A guy who'd do anything for a fast buck. "Did you tell Natasha—I mean Tonya, what you were doing?" She tried not to glare at him.

He cut his eyes at her. "No. She didn't need to know about my extracurricular activities."

"But she's a psychic," Deena argued. "Wouldn't she know anyway?"

He pursed his lips and looked back at Ian.

"What else did he pay you to do?" Ian asked.

"Just the thing with the bats. I told you about that yesterday."

"Have you ever heard of Jackson Oil and Gas?"

"No."

"Did Mr. Fisk ever mention anything about oil wells?"

"No."

Ian looked back at his notes. "You said you called him when you were in the parking lot of the pawn shop. Do you know where he was at the time?"

"Nope, and I didn't ask. He seemed plenty mad. Said he'd told me about leaving the box in the dumpster, but I swear he didn't."

"I'm curious," Ian said. "Why were you and Tonya in Maycroft to begin with? What did you do in Las Vegas?"

Deena was dying to hear the answer to that one.

"I worked the clubs as a magician. She...was...a psychic. We got tired of Vegas and decided to head to Florida. When we broke down here, we liked the place so much we decided to stay. That's it."

Deena wanted to say something, but held her tongue.

Ian nodded his head, and then reached into the bottom of his folder and pulled out some pictures.

Deena darted her eyes away when she realized what they were.

"Take a look at this picture," Ian said. "Do you see that black swatch of fabric on the floor? It appears to be made of velvet. It looks like it got caught in the door and tore off of something. Do you know where it might have come from?"

"No sir. It didn't come from me. I was wearing a black t-shirt. I don't think it tore, and it certainly wasn't made of velvet."

Ian stuck the pictures back in the folder. "Okay. That's about it for now. We're going to need to talk to Tonya. Verify your alibi for seven o'clock."

"No!" Roscoe said. "Leave her out of this."

Ian raised an eyebrow. "Why? What's the problem?"

For the first time during their interview, Roscoe looked nervous. He clenched his hands tightly. "It's just that she doesn't know about my deal with Fisk. I don't want her to know I was lying to her."

"We're going to have to talk to her eventually. I'll wait a couple of days to give you time to tell her yourself. Deal?"

"I guess."

Ian stood up and knocked on the door for the guard. Roscoe was taken away.

Deena waited until they were gone. "He's hiding something, you know."

Ian stuffed his notepad and folders back in his satchel. "I know."

"Do you want me to talk to Tonya before Roscoe has a chance to get to her?"

"We're the defense team, remember? He'll tell us the truth, don't worry. For now, we need to talk to Detective Evans and convince him to look into Marty Fisk."

Deena shook her head reluctantly.

Ian gave her a sideways look. "You're still on board, aren't you?"

"Yes. As long as this ship is headed for truth-ville, I'm on board."

# Chapter 25

**S**igns warning visitors that their conversations with inmates may be recorded were nothing new for Roscoe. He wasn't surprised that this hole-in-the-wall jail hadn't upgraded to video visitations either. The guard sat him down in the chair and stood in his spot against the back wall. "Ten minutes."

Roscoe was relieved to see Tonya in her Natasha get-up. He hadn't told anyone that she was a fake and was crossing his fingers they could keep up their little charade. He scooted his chair up toward the glass wall and picked up the phone. "Hey, baby. You look beautiful."

She was red-faced and spittin' mad. "Shut up. I can't believe this happened. What am I supposed to do? I had to take a cab over here."

"I didn't do it," he said. "I was just in the wrong place at the wrong time."

"Whatever." She glanced back at the guard. "Did they give you a lawyer?"

"Yes. Ian Davis. He's going to be contacting you."

"What am I supposed to tell him? I know what happened. I know you—" She lowered her head. "Why were you over there anyway? It was that girl from the other day, wasn't it?"

"It's not what you think. I told you, it was all a big mix up."

Tonya rested her head in her hand. "When are they letting you out on bail?"

"They're not. It's because of Vegas." He watched her face turn pale.

"What if we pay your bond for that? We've got a lot of money now."

He flashed his eyes at her, sending her veiled lies and secret signals. "No we don't, remember? Besides, I think it's too late now."

"Have you told your lawyer about our...business?"

"I told him that you are the most awesome psychic ever and that I'm so glad you picked me to be your boyfriend." He needed her to know he was keeping her identity a secret for now.

"I've quit seeing customers and don't plan to see any more until this mess is over with."

"That's probably a good idea. You know best." As much as it pained him, he needed her on his side now. He hated being in a position of needing Tonya or anyone. He felt weaker than the jail guard standing behind him, checking out his hot girlfriend.

"What should I do about a car? I have to go to the market and stuff. Do you know when the police will release yours?"

"I have a feeling the car is toast. It was held together with super glue to begin with. We can get another one when I get out."

She grimaced, her tone sarcastic. "But dear, I'm not going to schlep back and forth on foot waiting for you to get out of here. I sure don't want to waste our very hard earned money on cabs. The money *I* earned while you jaunted around town meeting women at bars and such. Just tell me where you put the money, and I'll take care of everything."

How could she have known that? Was she a mind reader? Had she followed him? He wasn't used to her having the upper hand. He managed a faint smile, even though his cheek stung from the stitches. "Check the top of the closet."

She went from annoyed to furious. "I checked the top of the closet, you lying pig! *And* the bottom *and* the drawers and every other inch of that rat hole. Now tell me where it is, or I'll go to the police and tell them everything."

This was a side of her he'd never seen before. He was grateful for the Plexiglas partition protecting him from her claws and fangs.

The guard shuffled his feet, probably impatient for the visit to end.

He wasn't the only one. "Now there's no need to do that." From the looks of things, he was going to have to trust her this time. "Check inside your tall black boots."

"My boots?" Lightning bolts flew out of her eyes. She clenched her teeth. "It better be there."

"It is. Trust me."

She rolled her eyes. "That's a laugh. Like I trusted you with that girl?"

Before he could try to defend himself, she slammed down the phone and stormed out of the room.

Helpless to do anything, he replaced the receiver. The guard took his arm to lead him back to his cell. His mind reeled. Just when he needed her, she had turned on him. He needed to fix this quick. Maybe it was time to come clean to his lawyer about everything. Especially about Tonya.

# Chapter 26

When she got to Ian's office after lunch, Deena had a buzz. And not the good kind. Her brother suffered from migraines, and she wondered if this was how they started.

Luckily, Rob had coffee brewing when she arrived.

She had stopped by to check on Katy at the hospital. They had moved her to a room on the second floor. The nurse said the doctor was cautiously optimistic about her condition, and they were keeping her sedated until the swelling on her head went down.

"Howdy," Rob said in a voice that was much too chipper. He eyed the skull and crossbones umbrella but made no comment. "We set up a spot over here for you to work. I put some basic office supplies on the desk. If you need anything special, just let me know. I don't know if Ian is going to get you a computer or not. You can use that file cabinet." He motioned to a five-drawer metal model just like the ones she used to have at school.

She sat down in the swivel chair behind the desk and almost fell over backwards. Being the new kid in the office was uncomfortable. It reminded her of when a new student would come into her class in the middle of the year and look so lost and sad. She wanted to see Ian's friendly face.

Following her nose to the coffee pot, she walked past Amy who once again was on the phone. Ian's cubicle was empty. She refilled her tumbler with coffee, adding extra sugar for a pick-me-up.

"Ian should be here in about ten minutes," Amy announced.

Deena walked back to Amy's desk. "Does he usually take long lunches like this?" She slugged down a gulp and burned her lip.

"He's not at lunch. He's been over at the police station talking to Detective Evans."

"Oh," Deena said, feeling a bit foolish. She tucked in her tail and crept back to her desk. The swivel chair was an accident waiting to happen. She switched it out for one of the straight backs, not wanting to end up going overboard. She pulled her notepad out of her black satchel, wondering what she should do. Amy and Rob were both busy beavers, making her feel guilty just sitting there drinking coffee.

Wanting to seem like a team player, she got up and walked over to Rob. "Anything I can do to help?"

"Not really. Ian will probably want to talk to you about the Trainor case when he gets here." He turned back to his computer.

Trainor case? Deena hadn't thought about the fact that the firm was dealing with more than one case at time. She wondered if Dan was going to give her assignments dealing with other clients. She couldn't believe it had been over a week since she had found Mrs. Wilde's body. She headed back to her desk and looked over her notes, wishing she were still curled up in bed with Hurley.

Everyone came to attention as soon as Ian walked through the door. "Deena, I need to talk to you. Rob, call the DA's office and see what they have on Raymond. Amy, did you get those letters in the mail this morning?" He was like a ship's captain, barking out orders to the crew.

Deena was secretly pleased that hers was the first name called. She opted to leave her coffee on the desk, but picked up her pen and notepad as she headed to Ian's office.

Before she even sat down, Ian was talking. "I spoke to Detective Evans about Fisk. He may be calling you later. He was apparently aware of his dealings with the neighbors because Mrs. Wilde had filed a harassment charge against Fisk last fall when he wouldn't quit calling her. It didn't come to anything." He pulled a stack of folders out of his briefcase and set them on his cluttered desk.

"So did he think Fisk might be behind the murder and attack on Katy?"

"He didn't say much, which is to be expected. He did agree to talk to him and check on his whereabouts during those two events. Problem is, if Fisk paid Travis and Roscoe to do his dirty work, he'll probably have a solid alibi."

That was the first hint that Ian might think Roscoe was guilty of attacking Katy. She didn't say anything about it. "Did you mention the neighbors and the realtor as possible suspects?"

"Yeah, but he didn't seem too interested in them at this point."

She shook her head. "Well, at least he agreed to talk to Fisk. That's something."

"Yes, and that's a start." He tapped his pen. "A lot is going to ride on what Travis is claiming as a defense. If he and Fisk were in on it together, he would have likely already named Fisk to the police. Maybe tried to make a deal. I didn't get the impression that Detective Evans knew anything about Fisk's possible involvement until I brought it up."

Rob appeared in the doorway. "Ian, there's a man here who wants to talk to you. Says it's important."

"Is he a new client?"

"No, says it's about an existing case, but he wouldn't say which one."

"Scan him with the metal detector, then send him back."

Deena's eyes widened. She had never thought a law office would have to worry about dangerous people walking through the door.

"You can never be too careful," Ian said.

The man was in his late forties and dressed in jeans and a cheap leather-like jacket. His work boots were muddy, and he was wearing a ball cap. He introduced himself as Duke Hambrick.

"What can we do for you today?" Ian motioned to the empty chair.

"I want to make you a deal."

"What kind of deal?"

"I'll give you information about one of your clients for help with one of mine."

"Let's hear it," Ian said.

"Not until you agree and shake on it." He sneered at Deena. "Does she need to be here?"

"Yes. I'm a busy man, Mr. Hambrick. I need you to be more specific."

"I got information about Travis Wilde and Roscoe Trainor."

"Travis Wilde is not my client."

"I know. I just came from there. His stiff-suit lawyers wouldn't even let me in the door. That's why I'm here. You see, I'm a bounty hunter. I have information about Travis Wilde's whereabouts the night of the murder that would clear him. Then I could take him back to Houston and collect my fee."

Deena felt like she was in the back row of a theatre watching a movie.

Ian was cool. He stared at the fidgety man. "And what am I going to get in return?"

"I'll tell the police what I saw when I was staking out the Wilde house this past Monday night? That's when your client got arrested for assaulting that girl, right?"

Deena jumped in. "Why were you watching the house for Travis on Monday night? He was arrested that afternoon?"

The man shifted uncomfortably in his chair. "Yeah, well, I didn't find out about it 'til I saw it in the newspaper on Tuesday."

"So, you're not a very *good* bounty hunter, are you?"

Ian snickered. "Tell me what you saw, and I'll consider helping you out. That's the best I can do."

"Fine," Hambrick grumbled. "I had been parking down the street from the grandmother's house thinking that's where Travis would show up next since he's originally from here. But the woman next door kept coming out and staring at my van, so I had to park over on the next block."

"Your van? Is it a white paneled van by chance?" Deena asked.

"Yeah. How'd you know?" Hambrick looked surprised.

"Keep going," Ian said.

"Anyway, about midnight, I see this car pull up just a ways down the street. This young guy gets out and walks back through the brush to the backyard of the house. Naturally, I think it's my guy Travis. He starts messing with the window so I move in for a closer look. It was dark, but the moon was bright. The last time I saw my guy, he had a beard. This guy was clean shaven and seemed to be a foot taller.

"I watched him. He opened the window. Something scared him and he fell back. He got something to stand on and went about halfway through the window again, and then it looked like he was blasted out of there. Glass went flying. That's when the old woman next door and her dog came out. I high-tailed it to my van and hid. Next thing I heard was tires squealing. The cops went flying past. That's when they must have picked him up."

Deena realized his account exactly matched the story Roscoe told. Maybe Roscoe was innocent. Or maybe he was going back to finish the job like Ian had said.

"We already know all that," Ian said. "How's this information supposed to help my client?"

"It proves he never went inside the house. He wasn't there long enough to attack anyone."

Ian looked at Deena then back at Hambrick. "The girl was assaulted earlier in the evening. Around seven. Where were you then? Were you watching the house at that time?"

Hambrick sneered. "A guy's gotta eat, right?"

Ian sat back in his chair and folded his arms across his chest. "I agree that it sounds like a good alibi for Roscoe, but if I'm going to talk to Travis Wilde's attorney, you have to tell me what you know about him, too."

Hambrick stood up. "If I do that, how do I know you will help me?"

"Sit down," Ian said firmly. "You're just going to have to trust me. If I think your story is believable, I'll get them to talk to you." He reached out his hand.

The man shook it and sat back down. "I was hot on Travis' trail on Tuesday. Last week, that is. The day the old lady was killed. I wasn't sure if he knew I was tracking him, but I knew he'd have to stop and sleep some time. I spotted his car at this shabby motel in Galveston. I gave the clerk a twenty to tell me which room he was in. Sure enough, lucky cuss was at the ice machine when he heard me knocking on the door. He took off before I could catch him. So you see, he couldn't have been in Maycroft killing grandma when he was in Galveston with me."

Ian seemed suspicious. "How do I know you're telling the truth? How do I know you'll follow through and testify to the police?"

"Guess it's your turn to trust me," he said with a sly grin.

"Deena, show Mr. Hambrick to the waiting area while I make a call."

She had no idea where the waiting area was. Luckily, Amy walked over and led the way to a bank of five chairs near the foyer. Deena wasn't sure if she should stay with him or not. She waited, thinking Ian would yell for her if he needed her.

A few minutes later, Ian walked out of his office and over to Hambrick. "I spoke to my colleague at Lyons and Sons. They are expecting you. Do you have a card or a number where I can reach you?"

The man pulled out a business card and handed it to Ian. They shook hands.

"Good luck," Ian said. "We'll be in touch."

They watched him walk out the door, ducking his head through the rain. He got in the same van Deena had seen last week around town.

Ian shoved his hands in his pockets. "You know what this means, right?"

"That Travis Wilde might be innocent of killing his grandmother?"

"And that our client might be guilty of murder."

# Chapter 27

**D**an sat in his Cadillac down the street from the law offices of Lyons and Sons. He was waiting for Duke Hambrick to come out of the building.

Dan's friend at the DMV was able to match the license plate number of the van to the owner and the county where the vehicle was registered.

After a little digging online, Dan was able to determine the van owner—Duke Hambrick— was a bounty hunter. Since Travis Wilde lived in Houston and had skipped out on his bond, Dan put two and two together to figure out Travis was the guy Hambrick was after.

Sure enough, a straggly-looking stranger came out of the building and got in the van. All Dan had to do was stay right on his bumper for two blocks to get him to pull over.

Hambrick stopped at a gas station parking lot and jumped out of his van ready to do battle. Dan carefully watched him approach the car before rolling down his window. "Hey. Dan Carson of the *Northeast Texas Tribune*." He held up his identification.

"A reporter?" Hambrick waved his hand as if swatting away a fly and headed back to his car, now dripping wet.

"Wait," Dan said. "I may have some information for you."

Hambrick didn't slow down.

"There may be some money in it," Dan yelled just before Hambrick shut his door.

That got his attention. Dan knew those magic words usually got him the information he wanted. He pulled his car up next to the van.

Hambrick rolled down his window. "Talk."

"I know you're a bounty hunter, and I know you're after Travis Wilde."

"So what?"

"I may have another bail jumper for you."

"I'm listening."

"Tell me why you are still in town with Wilde behind bars, and I'll tell you who it is. I'm just after a story. I have no reason to lie."

"Were you the one who wrote the story about the arrest and the assault on that girl?"

Dan nodded.

The man looked him over. "How much is the reward?"

"I honestly have no idea." Dan was counting on the man being desperate. Apparently he was.

"Let's just say that Mr. Wilde may have an alibi. Could be he's getting his 'get out of jail free' card real soon."

Dan shook his head. "Fair enough. There's another man in jail right now who may be getting out any day also. Wanted in Las Vegas. Roscoe Trainor."

Hambrick smiled. "Well, well. Isn't that interesting?" He closed his window and drove off.

DEENA WAITED AT HER desk while Ian took a phone call. Rob and Amy stood outside his office waiting to talk to him. The front door opened, and Dan Carson strolled in, water dripping from his cap and jacket. He looked like a wet dog. Just as she walked up to greet him, Ian called her name.

"Come on back," she said, taking Dan's jacket. "I'll see if Ian wants to talk to you."

Ian motioned for Dan to sit. "It's a busy day, Dan. What have you got?"

He laughed and crossed his legs. "It's your turn, remember? I told you about Jackson Oil and Gas."

"Let's try this," Ian said. "Tell me the latest, and I'll see what I can add to it."

"For one thing, I know that Duke Hambrick drives a white van and is in town to nab Travis Wilde and take him back to Houston. It seems Travis may have an alibi for the night of the murder."

Deena couldn't believe Dan had already uncovered that information.

"Impressive," Ian said. "What else?"

"Marty Fisk has an alibi for both crimes."

"You're kidding!" Deena nearly fell off her chair. "Where was he?"

"When Mrs. Wilde was killed, he was at home in bed with his wife. I thought for sure he would say he was with Georgia Parks."

Deena instinctively looked down at her boots, knowing they were hiding her neon purple polish. "What about the evening Katy was attacked?"

"He was in Austin at his daughter's drama competition. They performed *The Crucible*. Ironically, she played Abigail Williams. Their team won."

Deena's faith in her gut instincts started to crumble like a stack of fresh oatmeal cookies. "That doesn't mean he's not guilty of something, right? He still might have paid someone to do the work."

Ian eyed Deena. "I don't suppose you're talking about our client, are you?"

She scrunched her nose and turned back to Dan.

"The police questioned Fisk," Dan said, "and he sang like a canary. He admitted to paying Roscoe to scare the girl. That's it, though. Swears he had nothing to do with the murder or the assault. Detective Evans seems to believe him."

"How do you know all this?" Ian asked.

"Sources. Detective Evans may call you later, or he may sit on it a few days."

Ian grabbed his notepad. "So let's figure out where we are. First, based on Hambrick's statement, we'll assume Travis didn't kill his grandmother."

"That's a relief," Deena said. She saw the look Ian shot her and added, "I'm glad for Katy—I mean, Miss Wilde."

"Also, we know Travis didn't attack his sister because he was in jail," Ian said.

Deena tapped her nails on the desk. "We know Fisk has admitted to paying Roscoe to scare Katy. That corroborates his story about being there that night. He wouldn't go over there to scare her if he had attacked her earlier."

"You're right," Ian said. "If the police believe Fisk and Hambrick, that should get Roscoe off the hook for the attack on her."

Dan rubbed his whiskers. "Also, I can't see Fisk giving up the information that he paid Roscoe to scare Katy if he also paid him to kill Mrs. Wilde. It would be too easy to make the connection between the two."

Deena looked back and forth between the two men. "Are we saying that Marty Fisk, Travis, and Roscoe may not have been involved in either crime?"

Ian nodded. "It's starting to look that way. As Roscoe's defense attorney, it's all good news. But for the police—"

Deena smacked her forehead. "It's back to square one."

# Chapter 28

Ian was anxious to talk to Roscoe, wanting to tell him about Fisk and Hambrick. He and Deena headed back down to the county jail. They sat in the same room and followed the same routine of watching Roscoe be brought in to talk to them.

He looked more haggard than the previous day.

"Good news," Ian said as soon as the guard left. "Nothing is official yet, but it looks like Mr. Fisk may back up your story. He stated that he paid you to scare Katy so she would sell the house."

Roscoe raised his chin. "Hallelujah."

"Don't be worried if it takes a few days for everything to get worked out. You know how it can be."

"Thanks. Have you talked to Tonya?"

"Not yet," Ian said. "Looks like we won't have to."

Roscoe let out a sigh.

"You know that you're not completely off the hook. There's still a warrant out for you in Las Vegas. The Maycroft police will want to extradite you there."

"I know. I can deal with it."

"What about Tonya?" Deena asked. "Will she be going back there with you?"

"Probably. I don't know why she wouldn't."

Deena fumed, wanting to give him a piece of her mind. Maybe she would have to make another visit to Sister Natasha to tell her what kind of a man she was living with. Someone who would take money for unscrupulous reasons and then hide it from her.

Ian closed his briefcase. "Is there anything else you want to tell me before I try to work out your release? Anything at all?"

"No sir."

"Then I'll get to work on this and let you know as soon as things are finalized." Ian walked over and knocked on the door. The guard came in and led Roscoe away.

Deena stood up. "You know, that guy may get away with this, but he's obviously a criminal. I wouldn't be surprised if he ends up spending a *lot* of time behind bars during his lifetime."

As they headed to the front of the building, a sergeant stopped Ian.

"Hey, Davis. We had your man Culpepper in lock-up last night."

"What was it this time?"

"Loitering. He was sleeping in the park again. He left something in his cell." The officer reached under the front counter and pulled out a large paper sack. "Thought you might want to give it to him since it seems kind of fancy." He tossed the bag to Ian.

His face went pale as he looked inside. Then he stared at Deena with his mouth hanging open.

"What is it?" she asked.

"I don't know. But it's made out of black velvet fabric."

NEITHER SPOKE AS THEY drove straight to the office. When they walked through the front door, Ian announced to Rob and Amy that they'd be in the conference room. Apparently, that was code for meeting in private. He waved for Deena to follow him through the dining area into the kitchen.

It was her first time inside that room. A large oak table sat in the middle of the space surrounded by six chairs.

He pulled the contents out of the bag and spread it out on the table. The fabric was matted with mud and gunk. The smell overpowered the musty odor of the office. "What is this?" he asked.

Deena walked around to look at it from another direction. "It looks like a cape. Like from a costume or something."

"Check the edges."

When she spotted the ripped bottom corner, she held it up for Ian. "Ouch!" She pulled back her finger to see a sliver of glass sticking out. She leaned down to look closer at the fabric. Several small pieces of glass were stuck to it.

Neither said a word. Ian walked out, leaving her there with the curious garment. He returned with something in his hand and turned off the overhead light. He turned on a black light and scanned the cape. When he got to the bottom edge, there was a faint glow.

Deena had seen enough police shows to have a good idea of what they were looking at. "It's blood, right?"

"I think so." He turned off the black light. "But how on earth did it get in the hands of Sandra's uncle?"

"Sandra's uncle? Is that the man who was picked up for sleeping in the park?"

"I'm afraid so." Ian carefully folded up the cape and put it back in the sack. "Follow me."

Deena's mind reeled with this new discovery. For one, she didn't know Sandra had an uncle living in Maycroft. She thought she knew everything about her friend. For another, how would he have had a cape that might have been at the scene of Katy's attack? She assumed Ian was wondering the same thing.

They walked back to his office, and he stuffed the sack in the bottom drawer of one of his three file cabinets.

Deena sat in the chair, afraid of what he might say. What if he asked her to get rid of the cape? Forget she ever saw it. She'd be an accessory to something. Murder? No. A cover-up?

She held her breath.

"What I'm going to tell you is strictly confidential. I don't want you telling Rob or Amy about this."

"What about Gary? I tell him everything. If you don't want him to know, don't tell me."

"You can tell Gary, if you have to."

That was a relief.

"Sandra has an uncle who lives here in town. He's got some problems. You might say he's...troubled. He lives in one of those old motels on the outskirts of town. As far as I know, he's never hurt anyone in his life." He looked down at his hands. "I realize that the cape may be evidence in a crime, and I fully intend to turn it over to the police. But before I do, I want to talk to Sandra's uncle, Lester. That's his name. Lester Culpepper."

"I see," Deena said, wondering about the legality of sitting on critical evidence.

"If it turns out he's guilty of attacking Katy, so be it. But I need to hear his side of the story first." He swallowed hard. "I need you to find him for me."

"Me?" She immediately realized the error in her question. He had hired her as an investigator, and that's what he was asking her to do.

"I don't want you to do this alone. He hangs out in some pretty seedy areas. Do you think Dan would agree to help you?"

"Probably. I can ask him."

"The sooner the better. I'll make a list of the places you should look." He glanced up from his notepad. "And Deena, thanks."

She nodded. After he handed her the paper, he gave her a physical description of Lester. She walked back toward the kitchen to call Dan. As she waited for him to answer, she looked at the list. Two bars, three bridges, the soup kitchen, and a motel.

She called Dan and briefly explained the situation. He agreed to help her. As she picked up her handbag and walked out the front door, she decided it would be best not to tell Gary what was going on until she got home. Hoping for a quick resolution to this latest problem, she got in her car and headed for the motel.

Although she knew she might "get her hands dirty" in this job, she never dreamed it would be literal.

# Chapter 29

**B**ack in the Sixties, the Pine Tree Motel was an oasis for families who loaded the kids in the station wagon to make that long trek across Texas. A swimming pool with a diving board and a slide ensured parents plenty of poolside relaxation while the kids burned off pent-up energy. Today, the old place was best known for its broken neon sign that, when lit at night, read, "P-ee Mo."

That's where Deena waited for Dan to meet her Wednesday afternoon. She kept the car running and the doors locked, grateful it was still light out despite the overcast sky. She was relieved a few minutes later when he pulled up and parked beside her. She got out of the car, hoisting her umbrella against the light mist and pulling her raincoat tighter.

They walked toward the motel's office and passed a breezeway where several men were busy shooting dice and drinking from bottles in paper bags. Dan held Deena's arm and stopped in front of them.

Dan took the lead. "Hey, fellas. I'm looking for someone. Can you help me out?"

"That depends," the largest of the three said. "You cops?"

"Nah. We're looking for a friend. The name is—" Dan pointed to Deena.

"Lester Culpepper," she said.

The man snickered. "Not much of a friend if you don't even know his name."

Dan pulled a ten dollar bill from his pocket. "Would this help?" He held it up in the air.

"Well now, I reckon so."

Slowly, Dan handed him the money.

"He ain't here," the man said.

Dan stood with both hands deep in his jacket pockets and stared.

The other guy got the message. "He was headed down to the Oak Street Bridge last time I saw him."

Dan nodded. Deena started to say something when Dan pulled her toward the car.

"Thank you," she called back over her shoulder.

He motioned for her to get in his Cadillac.

Shaking out the umbrella, she put it on the floorboard next to a brown box. "What's this?" she asked. "Cassettes?"

He picked up the box and dropped it onto the floor of the backseat. "Eight tracks." He started up the engine. "We'll come back for your car later. And by the way, don't get too friendly with strangers. Did you notice the guy next to the wall pull out a switchblade?"

Deena's mouth flew open. "I guess being an investigator can be pretty dicey."

Dan moaned at her bad pun and turned onto Oak Street. "Are you going to recognize this guy we're looking for?"

"I think so. Ian gave me a description and told me what to ask him to make sure we have the right man. I'll do the talking this time. You watch my back."

When they reached the bridge, Dan pulled onto the shoulder and saw three or four men playing cards. "Give me your umbrella and wait here," he said.

"I thought real men didn't use umbrellas."

He cut his eyes at her and held out his hand.

Deena wanted to protest but could see the seriousness on Dan's face. She watched him walk down the muddy bank and disappear under the overpass. Every second that ticked by made her heart beat a little faster. Where was he? Why wasn't he back? She pulled out her cell phone and was just about to call him when the top of the umbrella rose up over the incline. Dan and a man that matched Lester's description walked up to her side of the car. Deena rolled down her window.

"Ask him," Dan said.

"Hi. Are you Sandra's uncle?"

"Yes, ma'am," he said, ducking down to get his head closer to hers.

"What's your favorite song?"

His eyes lit up and he spread his arms. As he started to sing, he tapped his feet in the mud and danced in a circle. "*I'm happy happy happy, happy happy ho—*"

Deena nodded to Dan, and he opened the back door. Lester danced his jig all the way into the backseat.

Dan got in and shut the door. He and Deena turned in their seats to face their new passenger.

"Hi, I'm Deena. I'm friends with Ian and Sandra."

"Oh yes. How are they?" His face revealed a near toothless grin.

"They're fine. Ian heard you spent the night in jail and wanted to make sure you were all right."

"I'm right as rain!"

"That's good," Deena said. She debated just driving him back to the office but decided to take a shot. "You didn't happen to leave something behind at the jail, did you? Something black?"

"Black? Now let me think." He scratched his beard. "Black...oh yes. I remember, now. That new blanket. Warmest one I ever had. I told Rudy I needed to get locked up again so I could go back and get it."

Deena glanced at Dan then back at Lester. "So how long have you had that black blanket?"

"Two days. Three days. Four. I don't remember."

"Do you remember where you got it?" she asked.

The man laughed and threw back his head. "I picked it up shopping."

"Shopping? Like in a store?"

"No. Behind them. In the dumpster."

Deena was losing her patience. This was like pulling teeth. "Do you remember where?"

"Oh sure. I'll show you."

*Now we're getting somewhere.* If they could figure out where he found the cape, she might be able to find more evidence from Katy's assault.

Lester whistled to Dan. "Go to that little store down by the pawn shop."

Dan headed that direction. It was only a mile or so away. He pulled into the store parking lot.

"Is this it?" Deena asked hopefully.

"Hmm," he said. "I'm not sure. It's hard to remember important things when I'm so thirsty."

"Beer or wine?" Dan asked.

"A little red chianti would probably do the trick." Lester's eyes twinkled as Dan got out of the car.

"Your boyfriend is a real nice fella."

"He's not—" She stopped, realizing the man was crazy like a fox. Deena was learning a lot about getting information out of people. She still couldn't get over the fact that Lester was related to her best friend.

Dan returned with the bottle of wine in a paper sack and handed it to Lester.

"Now I remember. Drive down this-a-way." He pointed down a dark side road.

Deena wondered if Lester was leading them on a wild goose chase.

"Stop," he said as they came up on an old office building with a "For Lease" sign in the window. "There it is."

Dan pulled around to the back of the building. "Are you sure?"

"Yep. I like this one 'cuz people get rid of stuff here, and it doesn't get emptied very often."

"Did you notice anything else in there when you pulled out the...blanket."

"As best I recall, something was wrapped up in it but fell out. May still be in there." Lester motioned toward the dumpster.

Deena looked at Dan. She couldn't ask him to do this on top of everything else he had done. She picked up her umbrella and got out of the car.

"Stay here," Dan told Lester, who seemed perfectly content to enjoy his beverage and watch the show. Dan opened his trunk and pulled out a flashlight.

The dumpster lid was propped open, so whatever was inside would be soaking wet.

"I'll do it," Dan said.

"No way. Just give me a boost." She laid the umbrella on the ground and felt the mist cover her face and hair. Luckily, this morning she had put on her low-heeled boots, which would make it easier to climb. She grabbed onto the edge of the metal container and tried not to think about the black slime touching her hands. She stepped into the saddle Dan formed with his hands and got her feet up on the side ledge.

Dan handed her the flashlight so she could see to the bottom. Wet boxes and old tree limbs sat on top of the murky sludge across the bottom. She moved the light around the perimeter but didn't see anything unusual. Breathing through her mouth to avoid the full impact of the stench rising to greet her, she wiped rainwater out of her eyes with a wet sleeve. She picked up one of the branches so she could push the boxes off to the side. When she did, something caught the light and reflected back. It appeared to be glass. She pushed again and it sank below the muddy surface.

"I'm going in," she said, handing the flashlight back to Dan. She put one leg over the top edge and pulled herself over, landing on top of a branch and turning her ankle. "Ouch," she yelled.

"Are you all right?"

"Yes," she said, rubbing her sore foot. "Flashlight." She reached up and Dan placed it in her hand. She took two careful steps toward the area where she had seen the glass object. Slowly, she dipped her hand into the black water and felt around. Her fingers touched something smooth. She prayed it wasn't an animal. She lifted it up. It was the handle to a glass pitcher. "I got it!"

A clap of thunder applauded her effort, and she hurried to get out. "Careful," she said, as she handed the flashlight and chunk of glass to Dan. She stood on the branches to get her leg back over, and Dan helped her out.

He was grinning like a fool when she landed safely on the ground. "I'm proud of you kid. I wasn't sure you had it in you."

"She brushed the wet hair out of her eyes and picked up her umbrella, puffing to catch her breath. "You know what that is, don't you?"

"Looks like the handle to the pitcher someone used to crack Katy on the noggin. The police never mentioned that they didn't find it, but they like to keep details like that out of the news so they can use them later to catch the bad guys."

"Do you think Lester did it?"

"Absolutely not, but let's get him back to Ian before he's too soused to talk. And if you don't mind, will you sit in the backseat? I don't want what's all over you to end up all over my car."

AFTER DROPPING OFF Lester and talking to Ian, Dan drove Deena back to the motel for her car. It was almost five o'clock, and all she could think about was getting home to shower before Gary got there.

"Tell me more about this cape you found." Dan wiped the windshield with the back of his hand to clear away the fog.

"Apparently, Lester pulled it out of the dumpster and used it as a blanket." She leaned forward from the backseat so she could be heard over the beating of the wipers. "He got picked up for sleeping in the park and left it at the jail. They gave it to Ian to return to him. The black velvet matched the swatch found in Katy's house and the edge had some blood and broken glass on it."

"So, whoever hit Katy wrapped the glass handle in the blood-smeared cape and tossed it in the dumpster."

"Right. And Ian is going to turn it over to the police."

Dan gave her a sideways glance.

"He is," she said.

"He better not tamper with it, because we're both involved now. I can hold off writing a story, but I can't withhold key evidence."

Deena shook her head. "Don't worry. He'll do the right thing."

At least she hoped so.

# Chapter 30

Deena slipped on her soft, thermal pajamas even though it was already March and the temperature outside had been steadily rising. She rubbed her wet hair with a towel after shampooing it twice to get rid of the sickening sewage smell.

Hurley, on the other hand, couldn't get enough of it. He lay curled up on the wet jeans she had tossed on the floor.

Gary walked into the bedroom. "Going to sleep already? Must have been a rough day at the office." His kissed her cheek and loosened his tie.

"Actually, I had quite an adventure." She told him about the search for Sandra's uncle and her Indiana Jones foray in filth.

Her cell phone rang. She had changed Ian's ringtone to the theme song from *Mission Impossible*. "Hello?"

She couldn't believe he was asking her to meet him at the police station now. It was cocktail hour, not criminal hour. She listened to his request and reluctantly agreed.

Gary frowned. "First dumpster diving, now late night rendezvous with the boss? I'm not sure I like this new job."

"It's definitely different from teaching." She grabbed the blow dryer and started on her hair. "You make dinner, and I'll be home in an hour. Promise."

THE POLICE STATION seemed less scary now that Deena wasn't a prime suspect in a murder case.

Ian met her in the lobby. "I turned over the evidence to Detective Evans and told him the whole story."

"About Lester and Dan and me and the dumpster?"

"Yes, everything." He stammered to get his words out. "I want to thank you...for trusting me and helping out today. It means a lot to me...and Sandra."

Deena nodded. "Are they going to question me and Dan?"

"Perhaps. If the evidence leads to a perpetrator and goes to trial, then you'll be asked to give a deposition. For now, they took my word for it."

"So why am I here?"

"They are going to need me for a while longer, and I wanted you to go talk to Roscoe. I called, and they said you can meet with him in the visitation room. Tell him that this new evidence is going to slow down his release. They have to check it for hair, blood, and fingerprints. Assure him that it will be worth the extra time since the evidence will further clear him of any suspicion."

"No problem." Deena headed toward the door, but then stopped. "Tomorrow, I want to talk about my job. I'm not sure—"

"You don't have to say anything else. We'll talk about it tomorrow."

AS SHE WAITED IN THE cubby on her side of the glass wall, Deena thought about what she had just said to Ian. She hadn't planned it. It just popped out. What was she going to tell him tomorrow? That she wanted to quit? Wasn't it just a few days ago that she was thrilled with this new challenge? Maybe Gary was right. Maybe she was looking for something she wouldn't be able to find.

A guard walked up with Roscoe and sat him in the chair across from her. "Ten minutes," he said and walked back to his post.

They picked up their phones.

"How are you doing?" she asked.

"Where's Davis?"

"He's at the police station. He sent me to tell you something. There's been a delay in your release."

Roscoe pulled the receiver away from his ear and shook his head.

For the first time, she felt a little sorry for him. His lips were pale, his eyes dull. She knew she needed to keep her emotions out of it. She signaled for him to pick up the receiver. "It's not that bad. You see, there's been some new evidence found that the police have to check out. Once they determine that none of your DNA is on it, they'll know you are innocent and let you go."

"What new evidence?"

"A black cape that was worn at the scene and the handle to a glass pitcher."

His eyes widened and the little bit of color in his face drained off. "A cape?"

"Yes."

"Black velvet?"

"Why? What is it?" This was not the reaction she had expected.

As though seeing a ghost, he stared into the distance. "Tonya has a black cape. And if that's hers, my prints are all over it."

"What?" Her stomach tightened. "Why would she attack Katy?"

"She was jealous. Thought I might be cheating on her."

"Might be cheating on her? Wouldn't she know? I thought she was a psychic?"

Roscoe leaned in and glared at her. "Oh, come on, lady. Everybody knows that was a con."

# Chapter 31

**P**reliminary test results showed no usable fingerprint evidence on the glass pitcher handle. Whoever had it must have wiped it off with the cape. Several days soaking in the bottom of the wet dumpster took care of the rest. The blood on the cape matched Katy's type, but would take a few more days to get a DNA match. Same for the hair evidence.

The police were surprised when they got a call from Marty Fisk Thursday morning. He told them that Tonya Webber had given him notice she was moving out on Saturday. The police didn't have enough evidence to pick her up without the DNA results. They needed a plan fast.

Ian said he wasn't surprised the couple had perpetrated a hoax, but if confronted, it would be Roscoe's word against Tonya's. Pretending to be a psychic was an invisible crime. As far as the cape was concerned, Tonya could easily accuse Roscoe of wearing it over to Katy's house as a disguise.

Although Deena could imagine Tonya attacking Katy in a jealous rage, she couldn't see her killing Mrs. Wilde. What would be her motive?

Ian, Deena, Detective Evans, and an attorney from the DA's office huddled around a conference table at the police station.

"Are you sure no one outside the hospital staff knows that Katy Wilde was transferred to the rehabilitation center in Dallas?" Ian asked.

"Unless someone squealed," Detective Evans said. "We made sure to keep it under wraps for her protection."

"What? I thought she was still in the Maycroft Hospital." Deena looked at Ian who gave her a sheepish nod. "When I called to check on her last night, they said she was awake. I was going to go see her this afternoon."

"She did wake up," Evans said. "That's why the doctor moved her to rehab. She doesn't remember a thing. Has no idea who hit her."

"That's good, I guess." The others around the table shot her a disapproving look. "For her sake."

"You know," Deena said, "It's an old trick, but it just might work. What if we have Roscoe call Tonya and tell her Katy is about to wake up and will be able to identify her killer? Then we follow her and see if she comes to finish the job. We catch her red-handed."

They looked around the room at each other.

"That only works on TV," Detective Evans said. "We'll have to come up with something else."

Ian's cell phone rang. "That's ironic," he said. "It's the police."

As he took the call, Deena watched his face fall. Before she could even speculate about what was wrong, he was up on his feet and grabbing his briefcase. "It's Sandra. Someone found her unconscious at the thrift store. They're taking her to the hospital."

"I'll drive you," Deena said.

When they got to the car, her hands were shaking. She needed to be strong for Ian.

As they pulled into the emergency room entrance, medics were wheeling Sandra in on a gurney.

Ian jumped out of the car almost before it stopped.

Deena parked and went inside. She could only imagine how Ian must be feeling. She spoke to the woman at the front desk, but was told she couldn't go back.

Too antsy to sit in the waiting room, she walked outside and took in a deep breath. The sun was out and there wasn't a cloud in the sky. The weather in Texas sure could change fast.

She walked slowly toward the front entrance of the hospital, her ankle still tender from galloping in the garbage. She called Gary, but it went to voicemail. No use alarming him. She left a message for him to call her. Feeling helpless, she'd have to be patient until she heard from Ian.

The automatic doors opened as she moved near the hospital's front entrance. She walked in and looked around. The gift shop was open, and a colorful spring bouquet drew her inside. She looked at the rack of greeting cards.

The automatic doors opened again. A woman walked in who appeared to be really, really pregnant. Like ten months. Her blond hair was obviously a cheap wig, like the kind you get with a Halloween costume. Women can spot these things. She wore a sun hat, sunglasses, and flip flops. A straw bag hung from her shoulder. The woman looked more suited for a trip to the beach than a trip to the hospital.

Deena's eyes curiously followed her.

Catching her shoe on the edge of a doormat, the woman stumbled.

Deena lunged forward to help her, but the woman seemed to have no trouble catching her balance. She made a beeline to the elevator.

As she walked away, something else caught Deena's eye. Hadn't she seen those feet before? That lime green toenail polish? Such a bold color.

It was Georgia Parks.

What would she be doing sneaking into the hospital wearing a disguise? Something was definitely wrong, and Deena needed to find out what it was. She ran to the elevator and mashed the button. With only two floors to travel, it didn't take long for it to come.

The doors opened to the second floor, and Deena caught sight of Georgia right across from the nurses' station. She went into a patient's room. It was the room Katy had been in yesterday.

"Stop her!" Deena yelled as she ran down the hall. "Call the police!" She crashed through the door to find Georgia, wild eyed and confused, holding a knife over an elderly, sleeping woman.

"Georgia, stop!"

"You!" Georgia yelled. "You can't stop me!" She swung the knife wildly, grazing Deena's arm.

Deena ducked and fell to the ground. Her handbag and its contents went flying.

A nurse opened the door and yelled for security.

Georgia ripped off her wig and came toward her again.

Deena wanted to scream, but fear had stolen her breath. She swung her leg, knocking Georgia off her feet. She grabbed the umbrella that had fallen out of her bag and swung it like a baseball bat, hitting Georgia in the arm and sending the knife flying under the bed. Deena saw her chance and dove for the knife. She managed to reach it with her fingertips, pushing it a bit farther out of reach.

Georgia tried to roll over to stop Deena. The extra padding under her blouse was too bulky. She tried to stand up but smacked her head on the underside of the metal bed frame. She fell back down just as a security officer grabbed her legs and pulled her out from under the bed.

Deena lay motionless with her eyes closed, trying to catch her breath. Her heart pounded in her chest, and she felt faint. She lay on the floor until the officer handcuffed and removed Georgia from the room.

"It's all right. We got her," the nurse said.

Deena opened her eyes. Her breath came in short bursts. She pulled herself out from under the bed, and sat up. Blood spewed down her arm.

The woman in the bed moaned and the nurse went to tend to her.

Deena's cell phone rang from somewhere across the room. She knew from the tone that it was Gary. She tried to stand up, but her legs were too weak. The nurse brought the phone to her.

Before she could even speak, she heard her husband's voice. "Deena, what's up? I just got out of my meeting."

"I...I just caught a killer."

A NURSE WHEELED DEENA down to the emergency room to get stitches in her arm. By now it burned as if squirted with a jalapeño pepper. She had also twisted her sore ankle when she fell, and the doctor wanted to get an x-ray.

Gary threw back the curtain as the emergency room nurse prepared Deena's arm for stitches.

"Deena!" He walked to her side and picked up her hand, holding it to his lips.

"I'm fine," she said. She knew he was worried now, but he would probably be lecturing her on personal safety before long.

"Hold still. This is going to sting a little." The nurse inserted a needle to numb the area around the cut.

Deena held her breath. Compared to what had just happened, this was nothing.

Ian walked in. His coat and tie were off, his face more pale than usual. "Deena, I just heard."

"Sir, family only back here," the nurse said.

"It's okay," Deena said. "He's my boss...lawyer...friend."

The nurse nodded and jabbed the needle back into Deena's arm.

"How's Sandra?" Deena asked, wishing she could drop Gary's hand to scratch her nose.

"She's got a bump on her head, but she says she's fine. They're running some tests. They think maybe her blood sugar dropped too low."

"Bumps on the head are apparently contagious." She pulled back her hand and gave her nose a satisfying rub.

Ian patted Gary on the back. "You have a real hero here. She's a keeper. I'll check on you later." He nodded at Deena and left the room.

She looked at her arm and cringed as blood dripped out of the gash.

Gary grabbed her hand again and tightened his grip.

"The doctor will be here in a minute to stitch that up," the nurse said and pulled the curtain closed behind her.

"I can't believe you ended up in the hospital again," said Gary, sounding more exasperated than worried. "If anything happens to you..."

"It won't. I'm like a cat with nine lives. Anyway, I'm going to talk to Ian when I get out of here. I don't think I'm cut out for this line of work. Do you care that I'm going to be unemployed again?"

"Absolutely not." He leaned down and kissed her forehead.

She filled him in on the details of seeing Georgia and following her into the hospital room. Georgia must have been in quite a shock to find an old woman there instead of Katy. Deena wasn't quite ready to tell him how scared she had been.

"Knock, knock." Ian stuck his head back around the curtain. "Sorry to interrupt you kids, but I have some news."

"What's that?" Deena asked.

He beamed. "Sandra's pregnant."

# Chapter 32

Gary was so glad to have Deena home safe and sound that on Saturday, he let her sit in his favorite recliner to prop up her ankle. Luckily, it was only a small fracture, but it would still take a while to heal. After sleeping most of the day Friday, she was anxious to re-evaluate her next career move.

She was glad when Dan called and said he would stop by to fill in the details he couldn't include in his news story about Georgia's arrest.

Gary led him into the den. "Hey, cutie. How are you feeling?" He took a seat in the easy chair, looking less like the rumpled crime reporter she'd let interview her at the hospital.

"Bored. Maybe I should reconsider quitting my job."

"No," Gary and Dan said in unison.

She grinned, knowing they were just looking out for her well-being. "So Georgia committed both crimes and then went back to the hospital to finish off Katy."

Dan settled back into the chair as if lecturing a college class on police procedure. "When they arrested her, she kept saying the collision between Katy's head and the tea pitcher was an accident. Claims she went over to Katy's to try to coax her into selling the house."

"Why would she care about the house?" Gary asked.

"Turns out, Georgia and Marty Fisk were having an affair—just like I said." He tapped the side of his nose. "When Katy didn't answer the front door, Georgia went around back and scared the poor girl. Katy tried to cold cock her with a Louisville Slugger. Georgia said she grabbed the pitcher in self-defense."

Deena scoffed. "If that's all that happened, she could have just called 9-1-1 and told them."

"That's right, but she was afraid they'd try to pin the murder on her—which they would. The two attacks were a little too coincidental."

Gary pointed to the newspaper on the coffee table. "You wrote that she confessed to the murder. How did they get it out of her?"

"That's a good one," Dan said. "She thought Fisk would strike oil, leave his wife, and they'd live happily ever after. It might have happened if she hadn't been so impatient. She was tired of waiting for Fisk to convince the city to re-zone, so she took matters into her own hands. She was always too cocky for her own good."

"I definitely got that impression of her," Deena said.

"She told Detective Evans that if she were going to kill Barbara Wilde, she'd have come prepared. She said she wouldn't have used a scarf the victim was in the middle of knitting. As soon as she said that, bingo! They had her."

Deena smiled and nodded.

Gary looked back and forth between the two and scratched his head. "But how?"

Deena raised her hand, reverting back to her school teacher days. "I know you think I'm a blabber mouth, but I can keep a secret. Even from you. See, when I found Mrs. Wilde dead, I saw the ball of yarn still attached to the scarf. The knitting needles had fallen out in her lap. Detective Evans told me to keep it a secret, and I did."

Dan gave her his signature salute. "Good job. That meant the killer was the only other person besides the police who could have known Mrs. Wilde was still knitting the scarf used to strangle her."

Gary clapped his hands, applauding Deena. "So Georgia committed both crimes, and the psychic was innocent."

"I wouldn't call her innocent, exactly," Deena said.

Dan laughed. "As it turns out, Tonya had followed lover boy the previous night to Katy's house. She thought he was sneaking over to the see the pretty barmaid. So the next night, she waited until he left and went over there trying to catch him. She got there after Georgia, but before Roscoe."

"That's when she wore the black cape," Deena said, picturing Tonya creeping around in the dark.

"Right. She walked in the back door and found herself in a pool of glass and blood, thinking Katy was dead. She thought Roscoe must have done it. She picked up the glass handle to get rid of the evidence and ran out of there. She threw the cape, the handle, and her shoes in the dumpster."

"So, what's next?" Deena asked, shifting in the recliner to try to find a comfortable position. "What will happen to Travis and Roscoe?"

She watched the smile fall from Dan's face. "The District Attorney's office is letting them both go. Duke Hambrick, the bounty hunter, is taking them each back to jail. That was his reward for going on the record with what he knew."

Deena shook her head. "And Tonya? What's going to happen to her?"

"The DA will likely let her go, too. They could charge her with obstruction of justice, but they only seem interested in charging Georgia for murder. And, according to his lawyer, Fisk plans to resign his seat on the city council and concentrate on repairing his broken marriage."

A hush fell on the room. Deena thought about Katy. Now that her property was more valuable, it would be harder to choose to keep the house. Maybe she could afford to have it picked up and moved to a different part of town. Time would tell. The doctors had said she would probably be back in a few weeks. That would give Deena's ankle time to heal so she would be able to help her new friend get back on her feet. Speaking of feet...

Deena's laughter broke the silence.

"What is it?" Gary asked. "Am I missing something?"

"I just pictured Georgia with her lime green toenails and bright orange jumpsuit. Bold colors for a bold woman."

"WHAT ARE YOU DOING here?" Sandra asked as Deena hobbled into the thrift store on crutches.

Gary held the door open and walked next to her to make sure she didn't fall.

"I was going stir crazy." She hopped on one foot and settled into a chair near the register. Sandra pulled her stool closer.

"But it's only Saturday afternoon. How are you going to make it another month?"

Gary pointed to himself. "You mean, how am *I* going to make it another month?"

"Poor thing," Deena said. "Sandra can babysit me for a while. You go ahead and get your car washed. Don't rush."

He hurried out the door, the bells jingling behind him.

"Glad to see so many customers," Deena said. "I hope you don't mind me being here."

"Of course not! I was going to come by to see you tomorrow any way." She glanced around the store to see if anyone needed help. A woman with a handful of clothes walked up, and Sandra opened the dressing room door for her.

"Does it hurt?" Sandra asked, motioning to Deena's foot when she returned to the counter.

"Not much, but I'm on pain killers. How about you? Any morning sickness?"

"A little. The doctor gave me something that's supposed to help." She rubbed her stomach.

The front door jingled, and they both looked up. The girl looked familiar, but Deena couldn't quite place her. She wore a t-shirt and jeans. Her dark hair was pulled back in a ponytail, and she wasn't wearing makeup.

Sandra gasped as the girl got closer. "Natasha!"

The girl lowered her head as she reached the counter. "Actually, it's Tonya."

No one spoke for a moment. Sandra looked practically paralyzed.

Deena broke the awkward silence. "What do you want?"

Tonya clasped her hands in front of her on the counter. "I...I wanted to apologize." She looked up at Sandra. "You trusted me, and I lied to you. I lied to everyone."

"I know." The tone of Sandra's voice made it clear she was not in a forgiving mood.

Tonya looked to be on the verge of tears. "I'm so stupid. I wish I could blame Roscoe—my boyfriend—but I was just as responsible. And you...you had so much faith in me. I wish I could pay you back, but Roscoe took all the money."

Sandra's expression softened. She reached over and squeezed Tonya's hand. "Don't worry about it. Just learn from it, okay?"

Tonya nodded.

"What are your plans now?" Deena asked.

"I'm headed down to Mexico. My uncle has agreed to help me try to find my stepbrother. It's a long story."

"Do you need money?" Sandra took a step toward the cash register.

"No, no. You've done enough." Tonya smiled sweetly.

She was much prettier without all that heavy makeup. Deena also noticed a twinge of a Southern accent.

The investigator side of Deena couldn't help but speak up. "Can you tell us how y'all pulled it off? How you made those predictions come true?"

Tonya's face reddened and she shuffled her feet. "Roscoe did those things. He would slip stuff in people's handbags, slash their tires, even go to their houses and...it's so embarrassing."

Sandra shook her head. "Do you know if he ever came here and banged on the outside wall of my storeroom?"

"Probably."

"I knew it wasn't a rat," she said, eyeing Deena.

Deena crossed her arms. "Oh it was a rat all right—just the two-legged kind."

Sandra turned back to Tonya. "What about the Coleman boy? How did you find him? Roscoe didn't take him and—"

"Heavens no! That's the strangest part of this. I got this really strong taste of candy in my mouth. I don't know where it came from, but it was real. I promise." Her eyes implored Sandra to believe her. "Another thing that was real was when I said you have a lot of spirits around you. Don't ask me how I know. It's just this feeling I have when I look at you."

Sandra shivered. "What do you see now?"

Deena started to interrupt. The last thing Sandra needed was more talk of ghosts and ghouls.

"I know this doesn't make sense," Tonya said, "but when I look at you I keep seeing a girl. A little girl. It may just be my imagination."

The front door opened, and a man stuck his head in. "Tonya, it's time."

"That's my uncle. I better get going."

Sandra walked around the counter and gave Tonya a hug. "Take care of yourself. You know where I am if you need anything. I hope you find what you're looking for."

"Thanks." Tonya turned and hurried out the door.

Deena stared after her. "Are you thinking what I'm thinking?"

"Uh-huh." Sandra touched her stomach and smiled.

The woman who had been in the dressing room brought several items up to the counter. "I'm going to get these."

Sandra snapped out of her trance and began ringing up the clothes.

"By the way," the woman said, "when I was in the dressing room, I kept hearing a weird knocking sound."

Sandra's mouth dropped open as she swung around to stare straight at Deena.

Deena laughed and shook her head. "I think I just came up with a suggestion for Mayor Thornhill's slogan contest." She waved her arms. "Maycroft: Don't get too cozy!"

## THE END

# Works by Lisa B. Thomas

### Maycroft Mysteries
Sharpe Image (Prequel Novella)
Sharpe Shooter
Sharpe Edge
Sharpe Mind
Sharpe Turn
Sharpe Point
Sharpe Cookie
Sharpe Note
Sharpe Wit
Sharpe Pain

### Killer Shots Mysteries
Negative Exposure
Freeze Frame
Picture Imperfect
Ready to Snap

**Beachside Books Magical Cozy Mysteries**
**(Co-written with Paula Lester)**
Pasta, Pirates and Poison
Actors, Apples and Axes
Grits, Gamblers and Grudges
Candy, Carpenters and Candlesticks
Meatballs, Mistletoe and Murder
Honey, Hearts and Homicide

Visit lisabthomas.com for the most up-to-date book list.

# Acknowledgements

Thanks to my friends and family who were patient with me while I wrote this book during NaNoWriMo, which is National Novel Writing Month. It was a killer!

A special thank you to my beta readers: Lindsey, Sarah, Robin, Marla, and Lia. Your feedback was invaluable. Thanks also to Susan at coverkicks.com for the beautiful design.

Most of all, love and thanks to my husband for making it possible to pursue my dreams.

Made in the USA
Columbia, SC
21 October 2020